Untold Messages
William Seraph Martin

Untold Messages

An Account of an Aquaintance

William Seraph Martin

Books on Demand, Norderstedt, Germany

Bibliographic information of the "Deutsche Bibliothek": The "Deutsche Bibliothek" registers this publication as part of the "Deutsche Nationalbibliographie"; for detailed bibliographic data consult the Internet site http://dnb.ddb.de.

Production and publishing company:
Books on Demand GmbH, Norderstedt, Germany

Internet: http://www.bod.de

ISBN 3-8334-5451-2

Contents

This text tells the story of two persons who met under
circumstances which turned out far from conducive to establishing a stable social relation. Whether their business
relation, friendship or love worked out has been told in the
following chapters.

Acquaint

Sebastian: This was the week of the book-fair in the near-by metropolis. Temperatures could be called cool, not cold; competing with clouds some sunshine still produced warmer temperatures overall. For the first time an elderly man visited some acquaintance who lived in the vicinity of that metropolis. This elderly man, a professor emeritus, was accompanied by his younger wife. Wife and husband were able to meet a number of relatives and other acquaintances who gravitated around the book-fair: Their son, an author; the son's ex-wife Laetitia, working part-time as a literary agent; his nephew; his niece. They all met each other some Saturday evening in a restaurant. There the professor's acquaintance Sebastian and his son's ex-wife Laetitia met each other for the first time.

See

Laetitia: Dear Sebastian, though we met during a dinner with mutual friends — among them my ex-husband and my ex-parents-in-law — I doubt you noticed me as you were sitting at the head of the table. Your eating was slow, your look attentive, but you appeared not very informed about any relations of those whom you observed, nevertheless in some way you seemed enjoying yourself.

Sebastian: Dear Laetitia, since I had to organize the parking of a car, I arrived a moment late at the beginning of the dinner and wasn't acquainted to some of the participants. Having settled the organizational matters, I enjoyed talks to my neighbors, watching the others submersed in having a nice evening during that dinner. But I remember you very distinctly because your seat had the most space at both sides and you spoke least with people at this evening; furthermore you seemed eating and moving a bit uneasy and you were wearing a lilac coat. Later, people told me that you were the ex-wife sitting in some vicinity of your ex-husband, the son of the couple — the couple, professor emeritus and his younger wife, who was staying with me. Saying good-bye at that evening, I now recall your ex-husband and you releasing me with a curt almost metallic voice of courtesy. Since my attention was occupied by many other things, I just stored these impressions.

Laetitia: The next day, Sunday, you were so nice to drive my ex-parents-in-law to meet me at my hotel. I remembered seeing you the evening before, the young boy at the head of the table, watching openly and eating slowly. Apparently my ex-in-laws had arranged our meeting in such a way that they could speak with me alone. Because you reassured them that you would reappear at the hotel in two to three hours, then you said good-bye and left us alone.
We talked about my new husband and that I successfully

promoted our new book at the book-fair, to which I had traveled coming from another continent. I was so happy meeting them again and they were so joyful to see me, that I just absorbed this exchange of carefreeness. As we took a taxi to some café, somehow I got the impression that my ex-parents-in-law had an especially high opinion of you, Sebastian. This arose my curiosity — my ex-father-in-law having worked in areas of applied psychology and as a professor for neuro-science certainly has some experience in assessing people's characters. Since you had shown them a book, which you just had finished without having a literary agent, they wondered whether I, as such an agent, felt able to promote your book. When I wondered how a boy looking that young could have written a book, they told me that your age actually exceeded mine. They were so happy with me, I was so happy with them, how couldn't I consent — but I wondered why they wanted to see you surprised.

Sebastian: Fetching your in-laws and yourself from some café near the hotel I already should have been on guard — your ex-father-in-law joked with me sympathetically and his wife also showed me an almost playful mood. For a talk about personal matters you seemed quite relaxed. I thought: How nice that matters so rapidly developed to their better side after observing you the evening before. Later I could remember that on this day you did not wear lilac clothes any more. As we were driving from the café to the hotel, you developed an impulse to tell me what streets to take, which you suppressed clearly perceptible to me.

Laetitia: Another couple, the niece of my ex-father-in-law and her husband were to arrive shortly. Therefore we waited in the car on the parking-lot in font of the hotel. My ex-in-laws asked me to give you my business-card, which had printed the words "Literary Agent" on it, this I did. You took it, read it, acknowledged it, and put it into your wallet without showing any visible reaction. I couldn't understand how you could react so unimpressed, other people would have looked happily or in awe to meet a literary agent; you just acted ignorant, unmoved as if you knew something no one else knew. As my ex-in-laws already had told me, and as I could see now for myself, you really acted somewhat out of the ordinary.

Sebastian: As you gave me your card I received your look full of expectancy indicating me that I was going to be surprised. As I read the words "Literary Agent" on the card, one secondary incredulous impulse was "Ah, someone who wants the money I do not have, so this is a business-setting here, not a social call. — Although judging by the atmosphere this resembles more a family reunion." Very strange, the more strange as they explained that you worked for your husband as an agent under your maiden-name. I did not want to embarrass you by asking how many books you have been promoting so far.

Laetitia: Sitting in the car, we were waiting for my in-laws' relatives to arrive — the niece of my ex-father-in-law, a young woman to whom I had briefly spoken the last evening at the dinner table, together with her husband. You spoke with my (ex-)father-in law in the front of the car. I enjoyed talking to his wife in the back. After some while, coming to the point of speaking of you, she moved, addressed herself to you in the front, and asked you what you were currently doing? After a moment's hesitation, you just drew a book from the side of your seat and showed it to us saying that your sister had given it to you as a birthday present. On the cover had been printed the title "Crystals: The Playing Ground of Electrons"; they had told me that you had been trained as a physicist. Although, as they had told me too, they had known you for less than one week, you already must have had an exceptionally good relation. Because she, with her Latin temperament, apparently exasperated by your indolence in unanticipated situations, out of the blue, almost imploringly stated that she liked you very much. You just continued talking about your sister without any reaction. Since we spoke a language, that in part might appear foreign to you, you could have misunderstood that exclamation, but then you wouldn't have ignored it so completely. You were also searching for words slower than before. My (ex-)father-in-law's wife repeated the sentence a bit more commandingly "Sebastian I like you very much! Don't you understand me?"

Sebastian: What a situation. — How to escape that game with social grace. Taking it lightly would insult a woman, taking it seriously could insult a husband. And her husband stares holes into the windshield instead of helping me, so it's a ruse, they are curious about my reaction. She poses as bait, he analyzes. — "I let that sink in. And then ..." For a moment I partly covered my face with the palm of my right hand. So I had halfway gracefully steered away from that cliff. As I later noticed, to my somewhat timid amusement, I had satisfied them by telling them effectively nothing. But fortunately they let me get away with it. Such tests or games provide some exhilaration on my side, but only after I have passed them — with some minimum of social elegance.

Laetitia: You didn't ridicule her, you didn't answer in a glib fashion, you spoke and acted authentically. That's what impressed me most; and you produced a secret, namely how you would react if you were unprotected and what did you really think and feel in such situations. Moreover, you just seemed unable to act surprised or be intimidated by any action, why did you act so unirritable and unreachable? We continued talking on the back seat, men on the front seats, until the relatives of my ex-in-laws, the niece and her husband, arrived. I had got another hint on why my ex-in-laws praised your poised manner of handling situations and why they already spoke of you as family only knowing you closely for less than a week.

Sebastian: After saying hello to the couple, that just had arrived, we entered the still empty hotel restaurant. The women leading the way chose a table at the window in one corner of the main room. Thus there emerged a very interesting constellation around the table: Since the women entered the restaurant first, they clustered near the window, the men formed a kind of protective area to the rest of the room. As the host, you smilingly offered me a place beside yourself, I wondered again about your affiliation to me, which must have taken place during your talk to your ex-in-laws. You spoke to the elderly waiter in his mother-tongue radiating an air of sympathy, which was returned likewise. The restaurant and its people seemed to make everybody feel highly welcomed and happy.

Listen

Laetitia: You see, as I offered you the seat beside me I had this feeling of ease and safety with you. I had noticed that your eyes never touched my body like those of so many other men did. Only once during that time I noticed you were looking at my face for a second. You felt like a natural part not only of the group around me, not like a favorite brother, but neither like a grand-father — I just couldn't sort you in — maybe you resembled, excuse the comparison, a friendly elf sitting beside me.

Sebastian: Due to some unpleasant experiences concerning men forcing their women out of some communication process, I enjoyed seeing three women talking in such a relaxed and naturally placid mood. Without any strain or effort this group of three women produced a persistent atmosphere of mutual understanding and diversion, without the slightest aspect of derision or competition. For me — and maybe for the two other men too — this gave a sheer joy of being only part of it as an observer. If I hadn't been wondering persistently about this strange mixture of your affiliation to me as a literary agent and/or as a person, I would have been floating with joy; thus I constantly had this semi-business mode of alertness and assessment working within me.

Laetitia: We had a wonderful time at that table. For years I haven't had the opportunity to so closely speaking to a group of people coming from the country of my origin, farther away from my origins than ever. Here, somewhere near a metropolis, in a country whose language I could hardly understand, where I have had no acquaintances except on business level, in a weather colder I was used to, I found a group of people from my country, with whom correspondence developed better and easier than I had ever imagined. All these people gathered around me could speak to me so much in my mother tongue. People, partly strangers, became more family than I have experienced it ever before. A place far from home had become more home than any other home had for a long time.

Sebastian: From time to time you tried to involve me in the talk, especially you clearly had the urge to explain language specific peculiarities to me. Up to that time, even close relatives hadn't shown their consideration in such an extraordinarily pleasant manner. You were performing the duties of a hostess, but not so explicitly on the other, married, men. Maybe because they were perceived by you as having a better understanding of the language in which you were speaking, maybe because you tried to show appreciation for me having a part in making this reunion possible.

Laetitia: Mostly we spoke about the peculiarities of the Latin languages, which in their richness of meaning give room for endless attentiveness and cautioning. Since you, as my ex-in-laws had told me, you too were born in the same Latin country and left it at an early age; from time to time I tried to make sure that you knew what we were talking about. Since you sat there so silently; as usual I mentioned, as a means of first cautioning, the existence of my husband. With reasonable people that assures a half-way acceptable line of communication. And as far as I had been talking about you to my ex-in-laws, I figured that this would suffice as a clear message.

Sebastian: What a seasoned business-woman, so socially apt, so elegant as she builds a personal relation first, then showing its limits by casually mentioning her husband and finally probably going down to business. Businesslike even in only mentioning your husband, not his name or further information, only communicating a social structure giving you the status of a wife. And how subtle at communicating distance and connectedness at the same time! How different can be seen cross-cultural styles!

Talk

Laetitia: After hours of sheer enjoyment, parting, we walked in front of the hotel. First, I said good-bye to my ex-in-laws. I had been so happy to stay with them and to talk to them again. The feeling of having parents understanding and not judging or lecturing you makes so much a difference when staying especially with them. You stood somewhat at the side, still the sympathetic observer who enjoyed watching others enjoying themselves, as my ex-in-laws already had told me. Especially the wife had wondered why you, as far as she could assess, had not had any girl-friend at that time. I chose you to say good-bye as the second party because, as my ex-in-laws had told me, by offering to drive them around you made that wonderful meeting possible.

Sebastian: At any time I expected now a business-like interrogation about my book: field, interest-group, number of pages, ... But you didn't bring up the matter of the book, neither your possible interest in acting as a literary agent of behalf of that book of mine.   Maybe you were still enjoying the atmosphere?   Therefore I decided to bring up this subject myself.   Since I knew about problems that could arise in marketing a technical book, I thought it prudent and considerate on my side not to burden you right away with obliging you to accept such a task just between hand-shakes.   So, as far as I remember, I essentially said to you the following: "I had some problems getting my book onto the market.   I wrote that book for myself.   Often quality sells with difficulty.   I'll first try to do some things with the book myself."

Laetitia: What a blow, you rejected me as an agent, why did you act so withdrawn?   What made you do this?   I just managed to answer that "I already had some ideas what to do with the book."   Then you engaged in some nice and considerate small-talk about my flight back to where I came from; the change of time-zones, stop-overs and stuff like that ...   You didn't want my services, but you returned my friendliness by most amicably speaking to me.   Why so much friendliness coupled with so much detachment?   What made you so interesting even to my ex-in-laws?   So, I would not see you again, I would not speak to you again.

Sebastian: The small-talk paused, indicating to say good-bye, I looked up.   You were scanning me in a most unusual manner — to my surprise — or not to my surprise.   You paused, and without saying a word asking me "I don't want to embarrass you but, please open yourself to me, tell me something about yourself.   I won't hurt you, may I step in for only a short glance?"   You insisted.   You opened yourself at the same time and showed so much of yourself that looking at you with a wide open eye could have been called committing an indecent act. You insisted to ask, did there exist an answer? What question? What answer did you expect? I carefully looked aside and waited for a moment, not knowing what to do or to answer. You approached me, embraced me carefully and said good-bye. Something sank into me, I remained just watching, wondering what had happened.

Laetitia: You just did what you said. You looked at me like a six year old boy without any male dominance or measuring interest, your eyes were so completely void of that kind of focus one often sees when men are looking into women's eyes or somewhere else. You lay bare, while not giving yourself away. You just looked, a childlike collector of sights, the back of your eyes tentatively questioning the whole world with an air of basic caring and steadiness that — at the same time — made your eyes look like that of an old man's.

Eyes like a flight of doors opening successively into a baroque château. Revealing an unfathomable depth and stunning beauty, a reflection of the invisible, a promise of meaning and understanding.

You stopped it clearly to save me embarrassment, not because you weren't able to hold that glance. I don't know what urged me to hug you. You clearly acted not in a way called sweet, but you certainly did not really compare to any other man I had seen to that time.

Sebastian: Slightly dumbfounded, I just collected further impressional thoughts. Strangely enough, remembering that situation weeks later, you seemed to have grown: You, in my mind, became a person at least ten feet tall.

Laetitia: As my ex-in-laws had told me, this was family, which I was in the course of leaving. Finally saying good-bye to the niece of my ex-in-laws I did not know what had got into me. I silently broke into tears, waved them good-bye and entered the deserted hotel-restaurant, rushed to the dead-silent hotel-lobby, got the empty lift and ran the corridor to my room, closing the door and throwing myself onto the bed, weeping.

Sebastian: Embracing your ex-in-laws' niece you seemed overwhelmed by emotion and waved good-bye to all the rest. The rest of the group stood there uneasily, wondering what just had happened. They dispersed with a preoccupied move. Each one so dumbfounded that even the search of an explanation bogged down.

Laetitia: Just leaving that group, which had visited me and talked with me, the ex-in-laws reviving so many memories, the friendly interesting other people I would have to leave, departing for another continent. Giving me an idea of peaceful carefree happiness after the cooler business atmosphere of the book-fair. Despondency and happiness mixed into one awkward feeling of a promise halfway held and then taken away. The travel, the change of time-zone all that moved past me without touching me.

Sebastian: The days after this, spent together with your ex-in-laws, distracted me a bit from analyzing my impressions. Then, I continuously kept trying to find explanations and clarifications for what had happened. Did I see curiosity at work? But what an inelegant way to try to satisfy ones curiosity unless based on some kind of panic. Posing questions "Are you what you seem to be?" in that way may provoke undesired answers with some people. Was this a game of the kind "How will he react?"? Game-players do not open their brain to such an extent. Game-players show unhappiness not so structurally imprinted. Game-players try to get control of themselves and others, they glare — they act sweet and coherently convincing — they do not ask questions with a plea in their eyes. If game-players use tears they don't show confusion what to do with themselves and then escape into the hotel-entrance. If this was another way of saying "Thanks for making that reunion possible?" this seems a rather unconventional, a most unusual way of formulation. Why not saying "Thank You" directly? As far as I know, you didn't raise children. Maybe, due to my outer appearance, you mistook me for a boy half your age? Did I see a surge of motherly feelings? Or do I look like your ex-husband, then why the interest clearly heightened only *after* your talk with your ex-in-laws? Did your business, though successful, turn out to have brought not as much success as expected and you felt afraid of not having any opportunity to return to the book-fair or to visit anyone of that group for a long time? What did you expect from me? If you weren't married, this incident would have been one of the cleanest, most sensitive and unobtrusive passes I have experienced up to that time. Were you partly unmarried already? Others acted like emotionalistic buzz-saws easier to fend off, you acted like a scalpel-sharp harpoon. Four days later I still wondered what had happened, before I found myself circling, even spiraling into a diffuse something of which I knew, that whatever kind of resistance exerted, it would end as a futile attempt of swimming against a tide.

Laetitia: During the book-fair there had been so many new impressions. The people of publishing-houses, new interesting books. So many recollections. Some part of me just was fixated on functioning in the presence. The past, so much reaching into the present, sometimes stifling and laying down borders that couldn't be passed. My ex-in-laws contacting me. Knowing about the presence of my ex-husband, meeting him at the Saturday evening without exchanging words. Why could I, with all my goodwill and my capabilities, and he with his favourable characteristics not manage to keep our relation a successful one? How could the quarrel about unimportant things produce such a devastation in every respect of our marriage? Why could such a strong protective cover like our mutual love cave in so completely? So completely that we can't speak any more, even after that time? (Moral rigidity, high standards, taking words literally to feel outrage justified, little mutual attunedness have been standard answers but that could not explain everything to me.) Where else could one find some dependability in life if not between husband and wife? Anyway, your look somewhat resembled that of my first husband and subsequently you acted aloof and distancing as my father. — And yet, your open eyes freed what you looked at. You could never act out a conventionalistic inquisitor. Sometimes I get the impression that many adults loose themselves in only recognizing and relating to their pasts; thereby shunning their openness to new points of view, and thus effectively abstaining from integrating new experiences.

Sebastian: Why did you attend the Saturday evening dinner in a lilac coat? Before your travels you knowingly bought or packed that lilac coat expecting to wear that coat when meeting your ex-husband. How did you manage to attend the family-meeting the Saturday evening, because it took place on very short notice? As far as I noticed, you did not speak a word with your ex-husband, both of you actively and closely ignored each other. So both of you exchanged some inaudible messages, both of you still heavily related to each other, although in a negating fashion. If you have that much sovereignty concerning your second marriage, why showing that inhibited, communicatively restrained, tense attitude towards your first husband? But that can change very fast as I have seen before with other people.

Laetitia: Then, at that Sunday, the first time having seen my ex-in-laws speaking so enthusiastically about a person. And that vexing curiosity whose immediate and longer lasting effects on me could have been misunderstood. But, judging by your look, you seemed fully capable of knowing what had happened to me. My ex-husband lost, my ex-in-laws lost if you spoke, my present husband maybe not happy with the financial outcome or else, and then me attracted by and attracting some unknown person. What a mess. What a price for a few hours of happiness. Have moments of happiness always have to be bargained paying such a high price?

Sebastian: Reviving that situation, I kept wondering what had happened? Apart from handling such situations chronically naive; often days after, there appears a nagging feeling "Was there something?". I think I was much too surprised to look at you other than with an initially blank-faced fatalism. But at the same time your face expressed such an intense feeling of apprehension, no self-pity, no depression, just communicating the knowledge of pain and a cloud of related emotions, that after three attempts of questioning I felt it indecent to longer hold that glance and, I hope I carefully looked beside your head. I wondered what you did want to discover inside me and what you had seen? Maybe people usually couple their perceptions closely to opinions and judgments which makes them a receiver and sender of preconceived views; I trained myself for more than a decade to break that line. As a part of that routine, the training comprised of searching for non-standard alternative inter-pretations of the situation as long as there is no imminent danger for ones well-being and health. Probably this and a natural tendency for acting with reserve hindered me from giving you the desired reaction.

Laetitia: This hurts. Another treadmill of deficiency — to be relived by thinking, never to be relieved. Another memory of happiness broken apart and true bliss turned into a ghost avenging the idea of life.

Sebastian: I remember, in that context, shortly after this, sitting in an Asian restaurant with tables built around a pool containing some fishes, I think Japanese carps and goldfish. A little girl was sitting on the concrete wall of the pond, stabilizing herself with her hands clutched to that wall. With a slight imploring air, she was begging in a low almost inaudible voice "Please, do not be frightened; please come to me; I won't do you any harm; I just want to watch you.". Then, waiting a while and repeating the sentence with the, for any onlooker clearly perceptible faith that her addressees will acknowledge her sincerity. I still would like to believe that the fish could have heard, understood her and have been able to act according to her wishes.

Letter about Games

Sebastian: Feeling deeply confused about the development, I carefully approached your ex-in-laws because, especially when contacting you after three weeks of waiting, I did not know how much they have knowingly taken part in mixing that up. I couldn't imagine that they would consciously arm you and throw you at me like a bomb. Naturally they kept very tight on giving information, as did I by only indicating involvement; so I observed attentively what they said and especially tried carefully to recreate what they had not said and why they didn't say it. But when they mentioned Eric Berne's book "Games People Play", this occurred to me as feeding me off so lightly, that I felt the urge to give them a clarifying answer:

Dear ex-in-laws,
thanks a lot for indicating to me the book "Games People Play" by Eric Berne. I have read this book in parts, but without having attempted a profound analysis, this book made me formulate some ideas: Saying of a person that this person (Berne-)played with other people gives me a feeling of uneasiness because in this case I would take the position of qualifying the other person as a whole. As a qualifier I leave the social balance. Instead I would prefer to use the word "game" or "(intuitive) game" for those social interactions of curiosity not knowing what effect to expect in advance —

without a planned definite outcome and generally happening in mutual consent. Because the idea of any child's play condenses down to intuitively obtain information or to evaluate information according to its usefulness. A non-Berne game also may feature characteristics as: Producing options in thinking and/or in proceeding. And above all, a non-Berne game may give an evaluation of, or help in evaluating, interesting constellations (Making any outcome secondary and not supporting a preconceived one). I think that another aspect of a non-Berne game discloses itself when loosing oneself in playing such a game. The following text tries to integrate aspects, which are useful for me, with my, I hope, pragmatic view that already gave me a tactical advantage in so many situations.

For me, the book of Eric Berne gave a list of interesting prototypes of social behavior and associated anti-theses for protection against them. Nevertheless, in the introduction Eric Berne says that usually only therapeutic situations allow to identify a Berne game. And if I recollect correctly, most Berne games have a protocol and repeat themselves in some way or the other. I think that this already indicates a significant difference from games of children or games of intuition of which one cannot anticipate these characteristics. As a person who needs to communicate with others in non-therapeutic situations, I have very little time to analyze the process and the actors when trying to react properly. The same applies to spoken communication, natural sciences or philosophy; also there, highly complex models impede clear thinking and appropriate reacting. And also when analyzing peculiar constellations within an entire social jungle, I cross known paths with interest, but I find it more interesting to orient myself using the rich signalization of nature and to develop my own intuitive interpretations. Thus I can discover paths which give me more information than I can obtain solely by recognizing prototypes or examples. Furthermore, matching observations and examples may insult or may trivialize the complexity of the actions of other persons. The models may give indications, but the primary source of evaluation presents the social jungle with its richness, from which I have to filter important and less important signals. Thereby using the idea of Carl Gustav Jung who, if I properly recollect a citation, said that if one has studied and analyzed the books methodically, then one should "forget" this background and one should use the intuition thus established.

Birthday During a birthday party, a girl-friend of Gamma had a jocular discussion with a man who tried to convince her that men were more intelligent than women. She, more intelligent (even on that low level of intelligence no insult intended) than this man, answered that women displayed a more complex intelligence than men. The man, not knowing what to respond, in best managerial attitude, asked Gamma: "And, Gamma, what could we answer to that?". Thus putting Gamma in a non-simple situation too. But, fortunately, after a moment's hesitation, Gamma's statement "I'm intelligent enough not to evaluate this question." apparently triggered a happily amused turn in atmosphere of the group attending this argument.

To give persons social liberty identifies fast some dangerous characters and friendly characters. Additionally, this freedom facilitates to see the variety of interesting social movements. Also this I enjoyed very much in that visit of yours; because in no situation, the Whole time, from No person, I experienced a dangerous or immediately problematic constellation. And I myself could take the liberty to react as I thought appropriately, I think without irritating other persons. In one situation I wondered what was happening, but I thought time will show. Then the following contact with you does not indicate a Berne-"foul", thinking of morals and rules, but "potential danger" or "social splinter bomb", as I could see a problem and I thought you could see the whole thing from a broader perspective and maybe could give me a hint for some specific responsible actions, if you found such hinting necessary. — In a group of Hippies I should have had no qualms about anything like that, because I had not to anticipate strict rules according to which people may act auto-destructively. (Actually even in such groups social relations won't reveal themselves as that simple, but this has been used as a prototype rather than a factual description.)

Discotheque Once a younger boy apologized to Delta; not until then Delta noticed that the younger boy had touched Delta's clothes with his cigarette, but without producing any kind of harm. Delta too felt confused because he couldn't assess fast enough if this situation could develop into a Berne game (with a hidden goal, even though the younger boy sounded utterly preoccupied). Delta's somewhat lame reaction consisted in reassuring the young boy that nothing had happened and that he shouldn't feel sorry. If Delta hadn't felt so surprised or/and so occupied to see any harmful or dangerous social context, Delta could have told this young boy that he should abstain from showing his perceived guilt so openly. Some persons would take advantage of his state of mind by increasing his guilt. In this situation a person took responsibility without existing necessity, thus potentially doing harm to himself. Even if there had been done some material harm, the damage could have been assessed less emotionally and a solution could have been found with both sides remaining calm and first surmising that each side would treat the other side fairly. (Thus humane behavior needs to hide when facing inhumanely acting persons and as a variation to this thought may be found the following proposition: Tolerant behavior finds is limit in intolerant counterparts.)

I, myself, use auto-destructive actions when feeling that these actions give an advantage in a strategy of protection or for signalizing empathy. But when I see such actions in other persons, where this occurs clearly without any strategy, but only out of an emotional impulse, then this gives me an uneasy feeling. For one part I remember being a little boy, and associating to the actions of mine a mix of curiosity, engagement and an idea of immense responsibility, sometimes thereby putting myself in insupportable quandaries, — insupportable for me due to the high demands towards myself — now I think not so impossible for others, because those others did not have an idea of requiring such level of sophistication, or they entertained an ignorant or tolerant view towards my efforts. Also when I can see tricks, I like to uncover an underlying strategy or a supporting point of

view.   And even if such an analysis turns out successful,
I still try to react apparently naive or I use other tricks
for protection.   Or if a manipulative course of answering
suggests itself, then I could try to reach a balance of interests.   And even if those tricks occurred as part of a Berne
game, which I could not readily identify, then such a game
would remain an unknown prototype and I would rather
prefer to keep agile by thinking of a simple communication
and how I can react efficiently to the "Signals People Gave"
to me.

Port Omega stayed at a port together with two girls. Both
girls knowing that Omega made it a past-time swimming
in cold water, they asked admiringly: "Omega, how can
you support that chilliness when swimming in those wa-
ters?" Having a hunch that this possibly initiates an uneasy dialog (maybe a situation of a Berne game) Omega
answered intuitively: "Oh, how nice, do you also see
that little fisherman's boat moored there at the pier!"
Without having some anti-thesis or some rule in mind,
this finished off communication completely, perhaps due
to inflexibility or due to the interruption of a protocol,
because Omega knew from previous observations that
these girls sported great skills in other social situations.

Reading the book of Eric Berne I think that there exists
an anti-thesis for Berne games, which works well in many
situations (without the need of knowing whether a Berne
game takes hold of a relation or not): First, maintaining a
pragmatic distance, maybe, if necessary, even with an air
of Machiavellian power-play (for protecting oneself).   Second, acting with confidence and humanistic inclination (for

protecting the others). Taken alone, confidence and human-istic inclination can result playing part in a Berne game of auto-destruction; they alone clearly do not guarantee a safe passage through the social jungle. Nevertheless these two skills form an integral part of most successful moves in the great non-Berne game of non-individualism. (Confidence and humanistic inclination to *oneself* relate to the themes of the books we talked about extensively. Relating to self-assurance, to trust one's hopes and ideas, to trust ones feelings, and to uphold a territory of self-respect that no-body may violate without identifying oneself as an unwanted person. This does not require to pursue violators with ag-gression, but maintaining the tenet that violators stigmatize themselves persistently and thus permanently leave any cir-cles of trust and confidence.)

For example, if I see a person who shows unconditional con-fidence in other persons, and if in this context that person feels completely safe with me, and uses minimal signals of defense, and at the same time signalizes a considerable re-sponsibility for my well-being, I already produce a careful line of reaction. I will collect signals for analyzing them, but also to store a reserve of information pre- or non-analyzed, non-emotional but impressional. Much of that informa-tion may allow an access to symbolical analysis by using a language, even if that may require to consider a lot of options. Without additional information even the range of those options may fall short of what comes close to an adequate analysis. Sometimes also independent inductions and exclusions give more indications. And at times, a good picture, that cannot give all aspects of a "reality", reflects the most important ones for the person who sees that picture. Like in other pictures I draw, I dislike putting persons into a classificational net or in any subaltern position, I can easily support this statement by using pragmatic and/or humanistic arguments.

If I feel confronted with curiosity, then I am careful not to use any anti-thesis, because in curious persons I discover myself, and although I think I use other methods to satisfy my curiosity, if it exists, I like to answer with tolerance but in a careful manner. Only then, if the opportunity arises, I like to answer with some curiosity myself.

In a pleasant atmosphere few people will present problems of their own formulated in language. Possibly because they also want to enjoy that atmosphere and so, if there exists a reason for curiosity, they might also try to see something. This initial curiosity might transform itself (seen as a process not as a state change). And if additionally one may identify a form of "sincerity of the moment", of which I have seen many, one should not mistake this as a game of any kind. This may give an indication of the person's perspective, but may not vindicate any form of qualification.

From inductive analysis using independent lines of reasoning and independent sources of information, I think that I can feel quite sure what I see in others. If there develops interest on my side, with people having lowered defenses, relatively fast evaluations turn out as possible. This I noted not only with myself, but also with people who have much more experience than I have. At some times I could inform myself whether my analyses came close to what other people had in mind or not; in most high stakes predictions, I was regularly confirmed conservatively, relieved and/or disillusioned.

Game "When I say I talk sincerely, I don't. — When I
say I talk insincerely, I don't." Since symbolic communication has its structural deficiencies. "Only if I do
not qualify my sincerity I talk sincere." Knowing that I
cannot communicate a total truth, knowing that others
are free to interpret my talk as they want to. But I can
have confidence in others, assuming that they see what I
say as an invitation to use their reason. Of course, there
exists an implicit supposition: The reality that interests
me is the one of my surrounding, not the reality of my
personal impression. Using only the reality of my personal impression can serve as the most effective means of
self-deception, in this case everything might become possible. That game forms a sort of extension of the Lying
Crete Paradox: "This is a lie." In a way this harshness
on oneself may find some reflections in the "Meditations"
of Marcus Aurelius I have read a year ago. And finally,
as positively as the notion sincerity may appear, sincerity takes no responsibilities for itself. Correspondence
on equal levels, openness, confidence and trust always
have to support a responsible form of attempted sincerity. Otherwise sincerity degenerates to attempted social
suicide, if not worse.

Method (similar to the book of Eric Berne, but disclos-
ing aspects of gaming with oneself) When I want to see
something in natural sciences or within social structures,
only auto-sincerity of the following form (meta-sincerity)
will help me: Doubting ones observations, especially
identifying interpreted impressions, applying scepticism,
inspect one's thought and tenets, compare different ideas,
find plausible structures and not to ignore the "impossi-

ble" constructs to get an idea of truth that includes the
point of views of other persons.   This forbids itself to
become any part of a Berne game, but mandatorily has
to become a game of intuition and reason (no hidden
interest, no anticipated goal).   This may turn out an extraordinarily difficult approach to get used to in the first
place, and even if practiced properly, this method gives
more pain than momentary self-assurance, especially if
one comes to the conclusion that things go wrong for
oneself.   But in the long run such a process gives an
immense emotional stability and a durable amount of
real security with oneself, not necessarily fun but a lasting emotion of the kind: "Now I can understand what
happened outside of me!" (The real basis of any natural science, unless one sees the necessity or is compelled
otherwise to spend a life-term in some established social
structure of self-deception.)

In several cases I could assess, the pertaining results presented themselves as I suspected only by using my intuition,
without extensive evaluation.   But those situations which
present themselves as highly complicated, especially those
of which one can notice that most of the partaking people
had basically different impressions, those situations usually
form the most interesting ones, often also the most stressful, stressful in various aspects.   But, if I see a game, if its
possible or adequate, I like to take an answering part in it,
not to merely join the game, but if possible to insert that
game into my method or my analysis.

Hotel At night, in front of a hotel, a girl approached Ep-
    silon.   She did not articulate her words, she rather pro-

duced strangely muffled sounds and tried to show Epsilon a paper with print on it. 'A beggar? An initiation of a robbery? A drug addict? ... ?' "Can you hear me?" She nodded. She presented a list of telephone numbers on her paper. In the following exchange of hand-signals, talk and face-reading, she indicated that she had been deprived from telephoning inside the hotel. And therefore she asked for a telephone-card to use it in the public telephone-booth in front of the hotel. (A mute person who wants to use the telephone?) Epsilon gave her his telephone-card and then he could watch with amazement how she produced a little keyboard from her bag, connected it to the telephone-receiver and thus could communicate via keyboard and telephone with some other person! As she had finished her call, she returned the card together with some money. Epsilon did not want to take the coins but she insisted, and Epsilon took the money knowing that thus she would not feel as a dependent person.

. . .

All the best, from Sebastian

William S. Martin, Untold Messages

Correspond

Laetitia: What happened? ... For bridging the first week, I can explain the altered state with the changing of time-zones and the stress of the fair and the traveling.

Sebastian: What happened? ... I should take some time to find out.

Ruminate

Laetitia: I don't know how these feelings can so strongly shade the years I have been together with my new husband, the times we have spent together, the happiness in some holidays, our work together on some pieces of art we produced together — all these memories now faded? He had helped me during the time when my first husband had left me alone; the worst of times I remembered — alone in a foreign continent, though feeling justified in my action but so very down — having to get a workplace and to make a living — how can this all become covered by just less than two hours of simply seeing someone? Even though we may have had some problems now, every relation does have its bad times, but that does not justify to run away, thereby severing all connections. What does that boy have except the eye of an old man and the promise of faculties I always wished to see in my partner? Why does just a moment of curiosity produce such a piercing inner conflict?

Sebastian: What did you want from me, what do you expect from me? You lived before, you will live after this incident, I did not see an acute depression in your face, so waiting three weeks before reestablishing contact may cool emotions down and give both sides time for coping with what has happened. Nevertheless, — day by day musing about what had happened, makes your grip stronger, especially as I am running out of alternative explanations, all of which systematically failed to fit into any coherent image. Reiterating the words "Why does she do that to me? She did not do anything to you — you are letting it do to you or you are doing this to yourself." did not help, this plea to myself actually only worsened the realization that something really had been done to me.

Laetitia: You felt like a magnet, this was magic how you could bind one's attention, how you could express something with so little — what you could hide behind the face of a little boy or not so little a boy. And yet, as I had been told, your age exceeded mine. I even didn't have your name, neither your address, no other way to communicate. I urged, longed to be able to speak to you, I even considered to ask my ex-parents-in-law for your address. After two weeks of feeling torn, I noticed what really did beat me up about you: Looking into your eyes and trying to see something, you just opened space for me, you allowed others to ensconce within yourself. You gave me an almost religious kind of promise, not worship; but promise of consolation, safety, dependency, understanding and overall warmth I longed for so much.

Sebastian: "Is nothing sacred any more?" I could listen to that stance till its ambiguity blurred out and recreated itself continuously. How can I respect their bond, in whatever form it exists, without questioning the newly created one, if this one forms a mutually accepted one too? Presuming a minimally working relation on their side this whole thing could end in disaster. Does she know how to handle those situations, does she have experience or skill in handling them and what would that mean to a new relation? Does she have the capability of balancing out two relations of similar kind at the same time? Can she accept two relations of a different kind at the same time? Therefore, if we should establish contact, this should happen using a very low contour to give her freedom for management. How will she react?

Laetitia: You commanded an independency and sovereignty so hidden, that exactly that act of hiding yourself behind the blank-facedness of yours made you so interesting to me. And judging from the stability of your look you did that hiding not because of fear from others but, as my ex-in-laws alluded to, from some strange foundation of self-sufficiency. Despite this, your look additionally conveyed an intimate feeling I only at times experienced with my husbands. This showed that, if you desired, you could leave that reserved status and I had the clear impression that you desired to take a step towards me.

Sebastian: Though, what you showed to me had all the characteristics of a clean pass, I kept wondering whether I should ignore your status as a married woman. Two hours cannot become the basis for a stable relation and if they incredibly do so, this time may have produced the initial momentum only. If this goes serious, then there has to come a process of careful balancing and scanning each other, to keep losses on both sides to a minimum. Not to forget the third side. But beside all that reasoning, you cast an iron grip into me. The first thought each day is you and the last one is you, I do not laugh any more, I have to fight that subtle air of fatalism. I cannot lunge out to you, I cannot stop longing for at least speaking to you again. An underlying agony seethes through the day.

Laetitia: I lost connection. People have changed, I have changed. The life I lived before appears unreal now. The short time away at that book-fair becomes like a year I have lost with my former acquaintances. Only parts of me live my old life. What promised to enrich life made my former life dull and empty. In the mornings I stare at the ceiling feeling like a block of concrete lying in bed, becoming a part of the space around me; in thought, I have to reassemble my body then, my movements have to be planned and finally executed against my body refusing them. I want to get out of all this so much and I want to get into it again; to enjoy some of the former old happiness, even if it may have lacked perfection. You just disturbed this by producing in me the conviction that there is more than I imagined to get out of my existence.

. . .

Sebastian: But what to do if this really gets serious? Go

step by step, do not let yourself hurry or intimidate, attempt not to hurry or to intimidate the other.

Laetitia: What should I do if you opened your world for me?

Contacts

Sebastian: — A Mail address had been printed on your business-card, which you gave to me while waiting that Sunday afternoon in the car.

Mail: Dear Laetitia XX, as told, I checked some further aspects concerning the marketability of my book. Getting an independent opinion on the quality of that book seems to really prove difficult. For example, at the end of this month, a magazine got a copy of the book and returned it immediately, refusing any further comment.
A first impression of the book could give an Internet-site. I would be happy if you could only check whether there exists any possibility for marketing the book in an English-speaking country. If by any circumstance marketing that book should produce similar complications as I experienced in the non-English speaking country, I should be equally happy if you told me so without pursuing the case any further.
If you needed a list of my activities concerning the marketing of the book together with a copy or copies of the book itself, I could compile the necessary information and send that collection to you by mail. Thank you in advance, because only the prospect of possibly writing this mail already triggered some

```
book-related activity and plans on my side!
All the best from Sebastian XY
(Interrupting some labor, the week's visit of your
ex-in-laws and meeting their family and acquaintances gave
me the impression of a holiday at home.  I have met only
very few people with whom talking and staying together
was so much at ease and so interesting.)
```

Sebastian: Having sent to you this text, I think, does demonstrate that you are in no danger of being badgered or stalked by me. You can answer on a business-level, on a personal level, combine those levels; or you might want to get rid of me right away, in case you perceive me as a danger to your life you have lead so far. To both of us, the three weeks should have given time to develop a working perspective on how to proceed in general. I should give you freedom to decide what kind of contact you wish with me. Thus the letter may appear somewhat indifferent, but I hope that its stance goes to the side of demonstrating sympathy. Furthermore, since I cannot anticipate whether or not your husband reads your mail too, I will try to keep my mailings as informal as possible to avoid any embarrassment on your side.

Laetitia: Mail coming from you. — ... — You write as if nothing has happened. As if you only see your book. Why can't you remain different? Why do you degrade what has begun, by acting as if we had a business affair? What kind of "sink in" did you do, and what do you really want from me? I'll wait and see if you mean what you say. Maybe you will not contact me any more. If I do not respond, then I know that you just play around and would rather hurt me than value me.

...

Sebastian: I should give you a time of at least three business days, so that you do not feel pressed.

. . .

Sebastian: No answer after seven days. What a horror, maybe I have pushed the case too far out by waiting three weeks. But that was no game. Why does striving for letting speak reason and respect dissolve into fright of having played a game with the other? A game that could have hurt the other. But whatever approach chosen, there remains that constant risk of harming a married couple.

Maybe that married couple is half unmarried already? But then I have to act with an extra amount of caution and sensitivity. I do not want to become responsible for any escalated quandary and finally taking the blame from you, your husband and your ex-in-laws for messing things up. But still, if you hadn't marked yourself as married, I could have been sure that you and your ex-in-laws tried to win me over. What a conundrum.

. . .

Sebastian: You gave me your business-card, I'll simply give you a telephone-call using the indicated telephone-number and ask. The overt measures often prove highly effective. But still I do not know whether someone can overhear the communication, so I'll take special care not to compromise you.

. . .

Laetitia: Your call. You acted doggedly. I had hoped and feared such a pass. But when I said that I had thought

about getting your address and phone-number from my ex-
in-laws you ignored it, even as I sent greetings to them by
you.   You just talked about your book but with an emotional undercurrent that made me shiver.   I was so dumbfounded, I merely managed to remind you of the existence of
my husband and then prayed to get that call finished.   My
ears rang after putting the receiver down.   So this was your
"sink-in" and "keep covered yourself" routine.   You did not
give yourself away.   I had pushed myself into your light and
you remained speaking from the dark.

Sebastian: I think I succeeded in making yourself feel re-
spected and treated as a person of equal positioning.   So
you knew I would not abuse whatever trust you had shown
me in advance.   If you perceived me as reliable and not
crossing social borders you would certainly become able to
tolerate me as part of your acquaintances and if there was
more to come, this could develop as slowly as you would
wish it to proceed.   When communication would become
established I could see what you really expected to see from
me.   Moreover I could not make out how the mentioning of
your husband should fit into that talk about my book? The
last time you talked about your husband, you hit me with
some machinations of yours about half an hour later.   The
happiness of having spoken to you lasted half a day — after
that — some nagging feeling took over.   Somehow I found
myself in a state of shock that you could intend to exterminate me completely.   Just as throwing away a microbe
in a test-tube after having looked at it long enough.   And
parallel to that, the other parts of the communication could
indicate what?   You pondered to get my address by yourself, for what?   You let me forward greetings?   And the

intonation of your language sounded miles away from any curt and professional handling of the whole situation. A shock, as big as the former one built up, in parallel: You were closer to me than I had imagined so far, the closeness had lasted! If you acted solely on that emotion you could bust yourself and me! So the whole thing has kept muddled up as before. I had to keep steering between two cliffs, without getting sunk myself by either one of them. — And worst of all, possibly even taking care not to break the cliffs themselves.

Mail: Dear Sebastian, here is just a short reply to confirm that I have received your mail. I'm glad that communications rendered OK now. I will endeavor to contact you through the current address which apparently works fine. I will look at the information on the web site you mentioned and return to you with some feedback.

Unfortunately I am busy this weekend as we are going away to visit my husband's parents, but I will contact you with some information by next weekend.
Best regards, Laetitia

Sebastian: How nice, but communications are OK by a sort of bullying on my side. I still tend to think that you act more interested in exterminating me than in developing any kind of relation with me. Fortunately you do seek some distance in time and social relation. So I am safe and we can keep communicative channels open.

Laetitia: I felt terrible towards my present in-laws. As if I was cheating on them. I became enjoying the moments with them and any other social contact, only not to become tormented by thinking what to do, how to escape that tearing of opposing obligations. I began intensifying my contacts, went out almost every evening with or without my husband, saw my friends. Only to get somewhere else with my thoughts. And this worked a bit, the perspective shifted somewhat back to normal. How can you tolerate me betraying you constantly with my husband? I have to loose that feeling of betraying myself no matter how I direct loyalties.

Mail: Dear Sebastian, I suspect that your book will be indeed a book difficult to market, because it is directed to a very small and specific target group. But, I do not know enough of computer programming to give you useful feedback, and therefore I sent your web-link to a friend who is in the Information Technology business for comments. It may take her a few days to review it, but I will give you more information as soon as it becomes available. Best regards, Laetitia

Sebastian: From my experiences here, I doubt that this will get you very far. But as I have also seen, sometimes the most strange ways produce the most stunning results. So lets see what happens next. Meanwhile my activities in sports have left me limping on one foot and they have con-siderably delayed my work. The chaos begins to pile up.

Mail: Dear Laetitia, thanks for the mail, it confirmed one of my reservations communicated that Sunday afternoon and reformulated in the first contacting mail. Nevertheless sometimes a seemingly unorthodox approach with people who acknowledge facts produces more stable or efficient results than expected.
If my activities here should yield some contacts would you consent to me transferring the data on your business-card to let them contact you? The attachment

contains a, hopefully incomplete, list of the book's
probably unique features. Maybe this could help a little
in germinating interest within potential clients.
Thanks so far, all the best from Sebastian XY
Attachment: ...

Sebastian: Another reinforcement for a hopefully poised
form of communication. This should indicate to you again
my wish for an equilibrated communication. But I will
continue to answer your mail within three business days
avoiding to make you feel that I have lost interest.

Laetitia: You constantly sign your communications with
your full name. Why do you show me that distance? Do
you need to hold the formal distance of giving me your full
signature because you are emotionally so close to me? I
always ask myself why do you have again so unconditional
a confidence in me. Each time you show this character-
istic, I fear to fall because you might step aside. Do you
treat me like a child that has misbehaved? Do you feel
any connection at all to me, except for that strange book of
yours? Am I the only one who thinks that something happened that day? Have I again given myself away to someone
who really does not care? How could you deceive me, how
could I misunderstand what had happened, waste my feelings on a nothing. I already have had fears of becoming
alienated to my second husband, have I been alienated by
you already? I just live outside of everyone towards whom I
felt attachment. This cannot keep up without ending soon.

Sebastian: As soon as you convince me that you will not try
to exterminate me or will not bully me again, I will sign my
mail with my first name.

Laetitia: I have fixed myself into that agent's business, maybe there is an easy way out. My husbands usually reacted and react very irritable to displays of ignorance and non-compliance, maybe you will too. I hope you won't, as much as I hope you will do. Maybe then, you show some emotions to me, of whatever kind they might be, I will just feel contented to see you wasting them on me. Why does any form of closeness always end up in having been proven to oneself, by voluntarily accepting anything good and bad from the other, why does this rout reiterate indefinitely?

Mail: Dear Sebastian, I am sorry but as a matter of fact I have not been able to do much with your book so far - looking at the web site I noticed the display of only an outline of what is covered in the book - would it be possible for you to mail a sample chapter, or at least a few pages of one of the most interesting sections so that I can consider going through them together with people working in the Information Technology business, thus becoming able to assess its contents better. I'm assuming the book is written in English, right? Please, let me know. I hope things are going well for you. I'm looking forward to receiving your mail - I'll keep in touch. Kind regards, Laetitia

Sebastian: Aha, "kind regards" and the first personal remarks. Either you are slowly establishing communication and softening up or you are letting me down easily. "I'll keep in touch." sounds much like "Never bother me again!". And after almost two months either you remain so troubled as to ignore the sample-chapter posted on the Internet-site, or you want to test me out: "Will he act enraged by my ignorance?" But if you tried to get rid of me by using such a simple ruse, I should actually fire you as an agent because of thinking that I am capable of reacting so intolerant, not because of the ignorance you displayed. If the atmosphere had not been charged so heavily I would have displayed a big grin noticing such a simple trapping attempt. So I just circumnavigate this by inundating you with information.

Mail: Dear Laetitia, time matters least, that book has been finished for over one year, so I am under no pressure. The book's ISBNumber was registered with the national ISBN-registry of my country. The authorship has been recorded under my name.
A hundred copies of the book have been printed in January of this year. A book-delivery center, contacted at about the same time, resented stocking these copies for direct access to the market.
The book presents its information in English (a non-English publisher asked me to translate the text to their preferred language before discussing the contents with me, which I resented due to the foreseeable amount of little-inspiring work without any guaranteed outcome). Another publisher told me that the American market for programming-books had ruinous aspects, I still cannot see how much of this may have a trait of counter-marketing. At the end of March I found an university book shop that took some copies of the book in commission --- the representative seemingly was eager to get that commission after he had inspected one copy for a week or so. Today I phoned them, and they told me that, so far, they have sold only about two copies and that other books sold noticably better. Nevertheless, he told me that, of what he had seen up to now, he considered my book far above the average level; and as I understood it, this was not meant as a consolation.
One university library willingly took a cost-free copy of that book, after inspection by some of their teachers.

Though many people in this country are capable of
communicating in English, there seems to exist a
tendency to prefer books in their own language. Maybe
the fact that you are active in an English-speaking
country could prove as a considerable advantage.
Nevertheless, as I said, if your activities should
render as frustrating as mine here, I should readily
accept a suspension or a stop.
Supposing that you possibly might have a slower
Internet-connection, I have added a xxxKB file to a
second mail, sent right after this one. That file also
contains a rather elementary account of basic object-
oriented features, preparing notions realized in that
programming language. Object Orientation basically
describes only a method for structuring program-code.
Proper application of structuring program code in this
way might give advantages when writing some larger pieces
of code (especially in a team). If you consider it useful,
I would send you one or more copies of the book by mail;
not mixing myself into your approach, I didn't want to
send you copies without your explicit consent. All the
best to you, from Sebastian XY

Laetitia: Thank god, that didn't work, but why does he act
like some little machinery again. He cannot be impressed,
enraged, saddened ... Why do you leave me alone. What
are you, on what could I depend with you, you act so aloof, I
never could see you. And in that way you would constantly
keep me in pain and insecurity.

Sebastian: I understand that you have to maintain a sort of
emotional hygiene but why do you have to sacrifice a complete business relation or a pure friendship to your present
marriage? Does this tell something about the strength of

your current relation? I answered you in a way that shows you that I see tricks and answer to them non-naively, at the same time retaining my sympathy although you apparently get harder on me, you seem willing to destroy the initial trust produced in that moment of closeness. Yet, you having much less direct experience with my handling of things, you trusted me so much as to treat me with extraordinarily friendliness and as to establish an intensely questioning contact scanning me three times on saying good-bye, embracing me. Taking into account the first letter, which got lost in the mail, together with our telephone conversation after four weeks: Why did your trust not persist in view of my defensive approach? Why do you need to choose between 100% for, or 100% against any form of graded sensible communication with me. A kind of love and sympathy remain, trust and the feeling of closeness would have, if ever to be reconstructed. How could you extend yourself so trustingly into me and then withdraw yourself so effectively?

Repulsion

Sebastian: I offered you twice to cut contact, just by telling you that you are free to suspend or stop the book-related activities. Does a feeling of obligation to your ex-parents-in-law hinder you? I doubt that, but what else could hinder you? Either you saw this as a bait and I haven't experienced you that playful. Or you just rejected that opportunity to bring down the relation for some other reason. You acted so introspectively, so self-reflexive that I doubt that any further interaction from my side would have had been given a

chance for stable constructive communication. Why? Can
you see in me a trait of irresponsibility, of inconsiderate egocentrism. Maybe you could detect some potential for such a
trait, which I myself haven't even noticed in me? But if so,
why didn't you cut off communication right away? Then
why did you hug me that evening? Only as an act of awkward relief of tension?

Laetitia: Maybe your look wasn't a personal look of appreciation, maybe this look was just a reflection of the humane
setting, which you could afford to place yourself into. And I
misinterpreted this as a personal interest in my person. What
a complete fool I made of myself.

Mail: Dear all, hope you have a happy Christmas and a
wonderful new year. We may see each other again some
time ... Best wishes Laetitia & husband's name.

Sebastian: What the hell did you want from me? If you
want to feel safe and again try to wear your husband like a
shield, expecting an attack only you conjure as imminent,
then I think I should reassure you another time that there
is nothing to fear from me, that I accept your status quo:

Mail: Hello Laetitia and husband's name, just the
evening before receiving your Christmas-email ---
pleasantly moved --- I read the last part of your
publication. All the best for you endeavor together ---
To you both the best wishes for a happy Christmas and a
bright new year, sends Sebastian XY

Laetitia: Mail ... — What? — By referring to our endeavor you allude to the happiest moments I have had with
my husband, you really insert yourself into my life more

than I thought you could. Its over. Now it neither does matter who let whom down. I found back into my old life. I have proven to myself that I am faithful to my husband by trying to push you away from me. If you are that good you will still like me, if you do not, I can rejoice in having lost you. Finally provoking you, thinking of you as a cruelly acting person, gives me the only way of feeling close to you, without indulging in unrealistic dreams. Even worse, these dreams would make me constantly feel as betraying my husband. Holding up an unfriendly image of you becomes the best substitute emotion for loving you. And now you even dare to shove me away more attuned to my needs than I tried that with you. What a unbelievable mess did I ran into! ... This gives a constant revival of the reoccurring nightmare of my early youth: Seeing some single, beautiful, slightly faded, but still colorful flower in a gray nothingness. But when trying to get closer, two concrete walls close in front of me, depriving me from looking and feeling, locking me into myself.

Sebastian: Possibly I intruded too much into your personal life by sending you such a Christmas mail? Maybe you mistook the word "bright" as a critique of your rather obvious sleight to irritate me by feigning ignorance and disinterest? Damn, if you want to see vicious moves in others you always find some signs of vicissitude; a (self-)destructive approach to any relation. I should accept the ambiguity of feelings that comes with this uncertainty and wait. Time solves many social ambiguities.

Laetitia: In the following months, only from time to time, after some movie, while reading a book, or just doing some manual work, the feeling of you shot into my mind. Recollections of my first marriage and you seemed not to compete with each other, but eating me independently from different sides. Memories, especially those connected to loosing people, triggered by small incidents now hit me unprecedentedly. You had not lived up to my dreams but I doubt that anybody ever can live up to another one's dreams. From time to time I feared that you had seen me as a crazy teenager who had to get some elaborate "letting-down easily" treatment. And I had thought I was letting you down easily. I hope that I had lived in your dreams, at least for a short time, at all. In that time and even now you probably felt no anger with me. How could you feel love then. Men, to my recollection, seem to couple these two emotions. Especially fathers, especially those who persistently tell that one acts socially deficient, and one tries hard not to, so hard that the hyper-engagement not to do something wrong turns all against oneself. I don't want to know anything about you anymore.

Sebastian: After three months without further notice, I think it appropriate to at least send a short notice, to reassure a possible personal- but not a business cutoff. I feel like I'm cooperating in you dissociating from me, whether I want to or not. But to me it remains hard to imagine how such an infatuation can change so effectively, without any social or basic humane bond remaining. Maybe you have distractions of your own (work, husband, friends) that effectively bar you from further indulging in these emotions of yours.

Mail: Dear Laetitia, up to now I haven't any special news about the book. Except maybe that a friend of my sister's,

working for a publishing firm, seemed to take some weak
interest. If something new arises I will give you
notice. I hope things have developed as you wished or
as you expected them to. So far have a placid Easter
holiday, all the best to you, from Sebastian XY

Laetitia: You left me as I wanted you to. But you left
me making me miss you and not making me indifferent or
reserved. At Christmas-time and now you present yourself
as a collaborator in ousting yourself. You make me feel sick
either way I imagine thinking of you. Sometimes I think I'd
like someone like me as my closest friend, who is married to
someone like you as her husband.

. . .

Sebastian: No reply. — Apparently you do not want to
speak with me any more. — So I think I can speak to
paper as well. — I wonder why there never occurred real
fits of anginess, the whole time I felt some emotional stasis,
a paralyzation, on a high level of agitation. The worst fear I
developed now was the inherent menace that you might not
live up to the sensitivity and intellectual capacities which
you showed me as we had met that Sunday. Compared with
your skillful appearance at that time, the mailings left with
me an impression of a most unbecoming and contrastingly
inelegant, almost compulsive, reactivity. I sadly missed
your social grace. But I suspected that you wanted me to
feel exactly that way to veer me off your track. But either
I was trapped again by form without content — which I
intensely doubt —, or as often to be seen in performing
arts: Depth, complexity and elaborateness hides well behind
apparent ease and simplicity.

Sebastian: Well, or rather unwell, I'll write down what I have experienced so far. And since things apparently have calmed down now, a written compilation of the entire process may clear up that confusion. A projection on how the other side might have seen the case certainly will widen my perspective on that network of observations and questions.

Letter about Methods

Dear K., remembering our conversation about how to treat people properly and how to evaluate their actions fair and unbiased for the good of both sides, I have compiled just some extensional thoughts that may fit into that topic and seemed worth adding. And my best regards to your husband who seemed to take great interest in our rather ardent exchange of thoughts and observations about the range of contents concerning the rather delicate topic. Your comments to the paragraphs below would find my most appreciating interest. I hope that at least some of the statements get accepted after having gone through your – as I experienced it – astute line of confronting them with real life settings:

You interrogated me about what makes a game differ from a method, and I think neither of us was truly satisfied with my attempt to clarify the difference. After some days of distraction I think one could condense down the difference between a game and a method to "cooperation" and "disclosure": In a game — at least eventually — the rules that governed this game should appear feasible to both sides. Basically games work between more or less equals who interact. Tests, clandestine manipulations, ruses do not anticipate the target person to look into their inner working. Even an approach to analyze simple impressions does not need to include the observed counterpart into the act of analysis. Methods either have a non-social character or need no disclosure if applied in social circumstances. But as usual, ultimate meanings become mostly determined by circumstance. — A method can be seen as a unilateral game.

observer Do try to watch a party of nicely laughing people. Or watch a group of noisy children playing at a pool-side. Living through some stressful period, one way of testing oneself for sociability just requires to watch a group of happy people and diagnose whether one can feel happy about them showing their happiness.

The following methods require a person to become active oneself, first on oneself, then on others: In feeling depressed or when feeling disappointed — for example due to one's own deficient assessment of a social constellation — you may get distance to yourself by trying to serve the emotional needs of others. Consoling others consoles yourself.

Professional bobsled-teams mentally run along their course before going downhill. Formation-parachuters practice their formations on the ground. Practicing oneself through a selection of difficult and reoccurring tasks helps also in new related unprecedented social problems. Also for fast and effective (re-)actions in social settings I have found previous mental conditioning an indispensable method. One may prepare and anticipate only few constellations. But experience-based intuition and alert observation often give hints on how to proceed with care, even in unforeseen circumstances.

cubicle For example consider a little boy in some pool-area in front of the changing cubicles watching a little girl speeding away from her mother into one of those cubicles locking herself in. The mother follows, and annoyedly threatens and reproaches the little girl while standing in front of that cubicle. What could this incident tell? First, having learnt from the action of the little girl, the observant little boy may imitate that maneuver the next time. Second, if that little boy imitates that behavior, tell him that his flight deprives him of a warm towel, a drink and the stock of cookies. After a time of exhaustive swimming that little child certainly will force himself into a highly cooperative line of action. (As usually, examples simplify, examples cannot cover ranges of complexities.)

In actions, the feeling of handling things consciously and remote-controlled by oneself often indicates a well-prepared safe track. That feeling comes from having thought through and having projected one's actions beforehand. From anticipating, dreaming constellations up, and asking oneself what reaction would fit into what situations, one eventually can learn as much as from experience. Projections and anticipations, repeatedly recalled, often transform into automated actions. What could appear as a wiser step in a surrounding that does not allow experimentation?
Observation and analysis require more time, more contem-

plation and more discipline, but if accustomed to and continually self-retrained to this methodology, one spares oneself living through many self-produced unhappy incidents.

entrance During a dark evening, in front of a public pool, a little girl waited alone for someone to fetch her. When I left the pool-area no one could be seen on the street. I felt sorry for that girl standing there so isolated and even in potential danger, so maybe I should have acted to protect her. How? Speaking to her? Asking her if she needed money to use the public phone at the end of the street and let her alone again? Waiting with her until someone arrives? Inquire inside the public pool whether there exists some authority who can act as responsible person? After the little girl told me that she had been waiting for a considerable amount of time for her parents to come, I decided to use the last mentioned approach for coping with this situation: I went into the pool-area, found and notified some responsible person of minor age! Returning to the little girl, she was now accompanied by a woman who had watched her for some time from the house on the other side of the street, this woman acted and spoke strangely.

I divide, as far as possible, feeling, thinking and acting, a hard discipline to uphold, but immensely rewarding, this saves others and oneself from despondency or worse kinds of suffering. Even with a considerable amount of experience, fast actions as well as fast judgments in new situations usually produce more problems than they solve.

eyes A three-year old boy didn't want to pass a glassed
path leading to a pool-area, insisting that there were glittering demonic eyes watching him. No one of the accom-
panying adults could see anything of that kind anywhere
in this surrounding. The little boy insisted and continued refusing to walk through that corridor. Fortunately
the adults did not force the child, but one of them lowered the head to the level of that of the child's. After
some moments of observing and asking, the glittering
eyes entered the adult's mind: Two lamps, positioned
approximately in head-height of the adults, produced
light reflected by the slightly unevenly cut edges of the
glass panes, so that — seen from a lower level — two
devilishly glimmering eyes stared at a visitor.

Especially if there doesn't exist an immediate necessity for
producing an opinion on something, one becomes free to
search for facts and inspect them. One allows oneself to
get time for building one's own perspective. And one lets
oneself convince by founded arguments of others, because
one has developed a good practice of convincing oneself the
same way.

Remembering also your remark on observing people, I tried
to rephrase your argument in the following form: Observe
one person handling third persons, especially persons whom
he or she normally would not assign great importance.
"Unimportant persons" make the most important testing
ground for one's own and others humanitarian instinct and
learnedness. Any subordinate, superordinate or peer, for
example clerk, customer or business contact, basically could
be treated like a subject performing only functional services,

but such a treatment would have a dehumanizing effect on social atmosphere and business- or personal success. Here again, properly balancing personal interests and social requirements characterizes the overall success of any social interaction.

The interesting thing to observe with fellow humans arises when assessing the degree of balance produced by the commingling of personal aspirations and humane views, in the perspective and actions of that person. Furthermore, one can consider it as a form of an art when feeling able to ignore overt show-like actions, but to receive only the little messages that tell about the perspective of the acting person. Like listening to the low tune behind the loud beat. The perspective of the acting person, as well as the effectiveness of the applied methods, both combine into a poised part within some group effort. One of the related questions wonders about what means serves friendliness; serving oneself or serving all the people present? A less differentiating view may wonder when the observed person changes its attitude "others are fellow humans" to "others serve as functional objects". Do own emotions define the relation towards humans? Does a person communicate sincerely hers or his own angriness or can the person hide such an emotion more or less effectively for the sake of all potentially affected persons? Do degrading actions of people produce solely a distancing, self-protecting reaction, without provoking the necessity of shredding the whole character of the degrader with some moral machinery? This culminates in the famous exemplary question: "How do they treat vagrants or other outsiders in general?"

Another standard method materializes when wondering how

persons react to unforeseen constellations, to unpleasant surprises, to stress? Do they blame, get aggressive, do they like to become outraged, lament, consider "If I/they only had. . ."-alternatives. Or do they introvert, feel despondent, wonder, consider thoroughly or search for reaction-related "Now, what if I/them do. . ."-alternatives? The "Why?"-approach, searching for insights and explanations, only forms a first step in that context. Here an arch-example may sound as follows: "How does my partner or I react if we get caught in a tropical rainstorm. Complainingly, accusingly or searching for some improvement of the situation."

Recall the example of the little girl locking herself into the changing-cubicle to her mother's great outrage. Observe how a purely moral analysis could vindicate the mother's reaction eloquently. As mentioned, that whole situation also allows a less twisted, a less warped view by assessing the setting and one's own options of learning which lead to effective counteracting. — The great outrage makes a rather ungreat method or even initiates a destructive game and thus degrades social relations. — So, in any social interaction I try to avoid any moral evaluation of the actions of others, I try to let my emotions not reign my actions, and to show a little bit of responsibility in my handling of things. ("No moral targets, no acting emotions, but a bit of responsibility") Even in certain unpoised situations this could couple with, as far as one's powers reaches, respecting the basic social needs of the people. Giving them a feeling of security, dependability, estimation or respect and above all: personal freedom. In the long run this should serve both sides! Nevertheless, if used sensibly the showing of some emotions may prove as a lever or as a probe towards a successful solution. Still, those people who do not get judged by yourself, perceptible to them, will usually react more accessible and usually non-aggressive. Thereby, one can better balance out the interest of different social instances, the partner, the group(s) and oneself. Many interactions may require to balance power, many interactions happen without anybody trying to establish a cooperative connection. Often exactly these settings promote the development of some social power-play. Happy may be considered those few who find a way to mutual cooperation or prove able to create a cooperative connection all by themselves. This includes, if necessary identifying, classifying and ignoring dysfunctional actions of third persons.

Some acquaintance of mine once cited the following sentence, told to him by one of his business partners: "If you let yourself goof you are worth being goofed." This may reflect social realities and many persons may label this as a true statement, but thinking and acting under any humane and cooperative impulse this statement may qualify as close to false. Like any good paradox, the statement itself, through its explicit content, forms a rather rigid warning sign and strives to caution others exactly from that to happen what it states so righteously. This forms one of those sentences one doesn't believe, because only someone with a respect for the addressee and with a basically good intent could be imagined to formulate such a strange attack. And especially here applies the saying that there exists no one more outraged about a perceived sleight-of-hand than an expert in ruses who has fallen victim to one of his own games. On top of all that, still holding his enigmatically saddened smile, this acquaintance added the following presumption "The best ruses strictly adhere to the truth. Because truth is what is least believed in.".

What has been stated previously extends naturally to any closer relation of humans. Some more articulate views of or steps towards a closer balanced social relation occur in the following order:

(Identity) Me and that person are made for each other, we are an identity by destiny. I live, I realize love. Its a spell that lasts forever and nobody will be able to break it, whatever may happen. We suit each other so well, we will never have a quarrel. I won't let go. I cannot imagine that I cannot have the person completely. I neither can imagine that I could destroy my private or public social image of that person, even if I deceive and degrade myself in that process.

(Bond) We are made for each other, we have the potential for becoming one. We realize closeness and love. If I cannot come as close to the person as I wish, I will urge that person to comply with or to understand my wishes. It could become a challenge to me winning that person over. That person changes my life, I change the life of that person; we both anticipate that change without expecting any major problems, because our relation proves strong enough. We can not only depend on each other, but we can overcome any kind of obstacle together. I cannot imagine to let go. I cannot imagine that I cannot have that person, and that I would not want that person altogether.

(Affiliation) The other one and I are different persons but we seem to correspond extraordinarily well, we have the potential for forming a cooperative union as well as we perceive the potential for leading successful separate lives, in any case even being able to support each other as friends. I think I can depend on myself, and I hope, that the other one can depend on me too. We can realize friendship, closeness and love. If I cannot produce any interest in that person concerning my person, I may coexist in its vicinity as long as either I have an idea of how to unintrusively interest that person in me or I wait until this person takes a natural interest. Awaiting an escalation through seeing, acquainting, communication and maybe more. Nevertheless, that person could become a danger to my peaceful life, so a slowly emerging relation should assure a kind of transitional stability, if needed. A first mechanism characterizing such relation consists of having the capability to get a distance to oneself and the other, even when in anger or indulging in other unconstructive emotions; and at the same time retaining the basis of mutual closeness.

Affiliation may include becoming able to realize aspects of bond and identity when serving one's partner's needs. One could hope that some people's openness makes them easily accessible to almost any form of establishing contact and even to developing a sort of closeness. From there to establishing a functional relation, it has to take some time and effort on both sides. Efforts and channels may take different paths and if these paths meet, its a particularly happy event. Time, letting things happen and to try nudging oneself and others inoffensively should suffice if both sides have enough interest in developing a relation. Chances usually occur in less than ideal settings, then other particularly civilized methods may take over, hopefully proving constructive in the long run.

Another mechanism and a really dangerous one, if invoked prematurely, presents itself as follows: Even if it would hurt oneself, but if it clearly serves the other, and if one takes one's own caring affiliation seriously, then it should become a possibility to let the other person go. So, if your feeling for the other has such a deep interest in the well-being of the other, then this could include the ability to either spare the other the burden of acquainting or knowing yourself. Since this method excludes the other person completely in establishing contact or a relation, such line of reasoning works clearly uncooperatively; this could produce more devastation and tragedy than imaginable. Therefore one should use that method with great care, this method can emerge as one of the heavy destructive swords of idealism.

pool-side Buying something to eat at the rather empty pool-side counter, I carelessly dropped the purse letting the coins spread themselves on the floor, it took me some time to recollect them. But, apparently the desk-clerk welcomed this as an opportunity to get into a longer extraordinarily sympathetic conversation with me, extending long over the coin-collection process.

In that context, make yourself aware of the need for adoration in many people. If you destroy what makes you adorable, you loose superficial infatuations faster than imaginable. Men proving weak or an resourceless idiot, women proving inelegant or clumsy. Superficial infatuations at best will develop compassion, but otherwise they let you subsist in peace.

But this observation also indicates the necessity of giving others their room in form of freedom and responsibility for themselves placing them into a status of autonomy and independence — and for laying off unwanted responsibilities oneself.

What about mind-cutting emotions of affiliation towards others? A feeling that might erase the present and the future, substituting them by a sort of purest hope. Even if that feeling makes the sun's glare a cold shower on your skin and makes you move in a trance; this feeling is nothing but an indication, a sign, not a program, not a strategy, it neither should account for a single action. This feeling solely may act as a trigger for investigation, for collecting sights and compiling insights. That feeling just represents the start of a developing relation, which like any process should not exclude delays or terminations (even if seemingly unimaginable at that moment). This indirect view does not destroy that feeling, but these methods rather protect this feeling from destructing itself and any person experiencing its effects. Here one may train oneself to identify those who make closeness a bonfire of emotions and living together a charred taste of hell. Then coming closer burns either them or you and nobody gets off that trip lightly. So, in these cases, you watch them, you adore them, but from a safe distance. Therefore real love hides and protects itself and both protagonists.

Statements of love in any form pose one of the most difficult settings to assess. An explicit form rather makes assessment more difficult than easy. Self-deception, short-sightedness and other obstructions may taint the pure sentiment, so the first assessment has to happen with oneself. And the second assessment may identify such kinds as sole lovers of love, beauty, complexity or lovers of power. Does that mean to act against nature, against any kind of evolutionary conditioning? Evolutionary conditioning, whether done by nature or by reason favors effectiveness and/or freedom to develop unprecedented ways of living in all its forms of appearances. Nature gives more freedom for development than human culture imagines. For example, mathematics in form of a human language learns heavily from natural sciences and vice-versa. So, acting according to one's human nature may well combine instincts with reason, culture with inspirations, or tradition with new ideas. This allows to integrate the diversity of different cultures and the freedom of thought, which nature has given to each human being, into a perspective of a balanced and satisfying interplay of one's individuality and identity. For many, identity seems to mean imitation and safety. And likewise individuality should not mean solely inventing and insecurity, failure and virtually never-ending agony.

Freedom of choosing one's identity or expressing one's individuality fuels hopes and self-given promises. But, in any of the then-resulting aspirations one should — at least — remain able to imagine the entire spectrum of results from unmitigated success to defeat and mischief and further oscillating twists the time-line may give to that process. All in all one can only strive to survive one's own life striving for a relative form of decency. Grandeur comes only with others who write down well-meant lines about someone else, usu-

ally thereby producing an unwanted mythology. Unwanted
by those who adhere to their experiences, their own proven
truths and independent aspirations, not to a posteriori- or
a priori-words of others.

. . .

Hoping to have formulated some helpful indications,
and sending you both my best wishes,
Sebastian

Meet

Sebastian: We have not exchanged any mail for months now. I have sent the last mailing unanswered by you. You did not explicitly cut the personal relation, neither the business relation. Although one could have understood your actions as wanting to draw yourself out of that predicament without producing any irreversibilities: Were your reasons only of self-protective nature; to let the hope of the other wither away? Or was it your own hope you wanted to see slowly draining away and at the same time testing the other's tenacity or tolerance? Who should be kept hoping? You or I? You certainly had acted out of curiosity, now so do I. How could I reestablish a contact, that tells me something? Should I give you a softer protective conserving contour as I have done up to now? Or should I change my strategy and enter your territory more direct as I did responding to your Christmas mail? Do I do this out of curiosity or out of what? What happens if you react different from just establishing a communicative bond, if you cut or glue, sever or attach, explode or match?

Or worst of all, do I see you as a great game? Do I solely train my hunting down technique on you? Does my capability of reasoning myself through such kinds of social spaces make me emotionally unfit for giving a poised reaction, or does this particularly qualify me to interact? Neither of the two options comes close to giving any help. Thinking about my motives is one thing, considering your situation and your understanding of it makes this really difficult. And should I therefore let you in peace? Is that peace the peace you chose and you desire? Can some form of contact with me give you another, better peace of mind? To what extent can I take a fair part in that decision? Would you live up to my expectations, and what if yes or what if not?

My musing should fade down in that moment in which I get the impression that this returns not enough new and feasible information. Otherwise one gets lost in spiraling thoughts constantly revisiting the same mental pictures. Fact One: You offered to act as my agent! Fact Two: I should feel free to contact my agent as I think it becomes necessary, only until that agent explicitly refuses to service me! Fact Three: There clearly exist unspoken social signals, not honoring them may rightfully appear as a breach of freedom and privacy of the other person.

But these facts do not suggest a sole choice between withering away into nothingness or bullying one's way onto the territory of the other one. There should exist many other ways, particular civilized ones for reestablishing an obligation-free contact. — Damn it, I just want a communicational contact, I do not want to take over the whole person, so why all that ruminating around?

Last evening I took a walk along a creek bounded by grassland and trees, again shifting and combining observations, notions, concepts, ideas ... Doing this, I lost myself so much in thought, that I hardly noticed the reverberating ground movements under my feet. A cracking noise and wooden slivers produced a turmoil behind my back. This only gradually entered my consciousness. Still somewhat dumbfounded, I slowly turned around and saw flying leaves, shivering twigs, vibrating branches and the trunk of a tree lying there horizontally. Something had happened. All this about ten steps short of the path I had gone so far. At that place, there really had existed no reasoning any more; and though I found myself somewhere else, this incident stopped thinking for a while. The rest of the brink of the wood nearby remained untouched. Leaves moved individually in the wind, together forming a glittering silvery texture. The setting of the sun turned this into a wallowing reflecting tissue covering, protecting the wood. Beauty and danger, harmony and loss all together.

Laetitia: At first I feared you would stalk me and degrade everything I saw in you, this fear took turns with hoping that you might come up with some ingenuity of yours, magically resolving this mess. Parallel to this, my anger about you ridiculing me by telling me that I used an "unorthodox approach" and wishing my husband and me a "bright new year", this anger immaterialized fast. Every try to construct justifications to see you in some unwelcome air failed miraculously. In hindsight I still wondered if it was me or if it was your strange book that gave you such impetus? If it was only the book, why have you been so considerate in offering to free me from any obligations? If it was me, why were you so inconsiderate to give me no clear reassurance of your feelings towards me? Were you afraid? I do not think so. Did you want to protect me? Why didn't you vanish right away? But you really continually practiced

what you showed on that deplorable Sunday of mine: You
let the other one sink into yourself like into a bog, and you
do not give the person free; while at the same time emotionally blackening yourself out.   You gave the other a friendly
warm impression, made the other feel safe with you, but
either you did some redrawing or you never gave yourself
away.   You just kept yourself under cover, protected as you
had indicated that Sunday by covering part of your face
with your palm.   Types like you wash people away like a
giant wave and then dissolve into harmless ripples of water
on the beach, — and yet your eyes talked ...

Sebastian: The next morning after the infamous tree-fall
incident, I felt venturing to contact you might beat my in-
troversion.   Come whatever will.   Since you offered yourself
as a literary agent I will send you *this* text for consideration
about publishing it.   Risking to loose you as a potential
acquaintance, which already may have happened.   Possibly
endangering your marriage, but I should not overrate my
influence or my power!   And above all, would my action
make you or me happier in view of a longer term?   But
this action certainly could give both of us a more interesting experience concerning the wealth of reactions produced
by human nature.   — Although I again suspect that this
"wealth" may rather singularize itself into a clean cut off or
boil down into a condescendingly cold-mooded disinterested
exchange of irrelevant words.   Another reason against sending you this work: Any cooperative reaction from your side
could be misunderstood as a confirmation of the contents of
this text.   — Checkmate by reason!   But why do I have to
anticipate knowing things about you, which even you do not
seem to know about yourself?   And what if my reasoning

was wrong? And again, if that text got into the hands of your husband, the whole thing could at worst mean doom for all of us. And yet, you used your freedom, so I should give you a freedom of choice too.

Mail: Dear Laetitia, I have sent to you, to hands of your person, the present text here in the name of my pseudonym. So, as my agent, you may consider whether this may qualify as fit for publication. All the best from Sebastian XY.

Sebastian: "Sebastian" without surname would have indicated an unwanted change of perspective. I hope all in all my communication reflected and reflects my feelings, it should address the friendly in a friendly way and in case there exist some doubtable views straightforwardly deflect them.

Conflict

Laetitia: A package from Sebastian, I thought all is over, now this starts all over again. ...

Laetitia: What is that ...

"Untold Messages, An Account of an Aquaintance. This text tells the story of two persons ..." ... **"Sebastian: This was the week of the book-fair in ..."** ... **"The next day, Sunday, you were so nice to drive my ex- ..."** I'll have to destroy this fast. ... How unrealistic. ... That is not true! ... What a dreamer. ... How does that end? ...

. . .

Laetitia: How can you dare to send such an account to me. If my husband sees this, then I'm in trouble. I should tell you in person what I think of that, and finish that whole thing off. I will say you firm and hard that you . . . — that whatever a relation we had — it is over and that you are supposed to never contact me again.

Laetitia: "Hello Sebastian, is that you at the telephone? You are endangering my marriage how can you dare even plan to publish such an account!"
Sebastian: "Hello Laetitia, its nice speaking to you again after such a long time. So you have read it, . . ."
Laetitia: "If you do not know what to do, better do nothing! It may take a woman to boil shit up, but it takes little boys to let it explode like a bomb! What a shamelessness on your side! . . ."
Sebastian: "Apart from the fact that I tried actively to eradicate any form of shame from my traits of character, I think that I'm not speaking to an expert in that field of avoiding, don't I?"
Telephone Receiver: "Wham."

Laetitia: So, he can speak to himself on the phone. This call was cheap and short. My ex-in-laws didn't contact me, you waited three weeks, I felt completely alone. Only my husband was there. So what do you show me, what do you expect me to show? Indifference, trust, surrender, non-existence? Little boys always manage to walk between your feet and trip you up.

Sebastian: Damn, damn, damn; always this big-mouthed sarcasm, I should have kept the contour broad, let her walk over me to see where she wants to go! Now the whole thing clearly has been severed off by my idiotic approach!

Laetitia: Why do I have the feeling that I always make you outsmart me. As if I have some masochistic tendency to elevate you over myself. And then let you crash onto me. This makes all so impossible. Why you, how can you know? How can you project, why can you write such a self-fulfilling prophesy? I will stop to make this naive set self-fulfilling ...

Mail: Sebastian, what I have done to you that you do that to me?

Sebastian: I am sorry but leveling this whole thing to eyesight I could ask the same question. I changed some of the settings to anonymize the entire process. I could have drawn clearer and harder conclusions from some observations. You didn't want to talk with me, so I tried to talk to myself. And frankly I couldn't resist the temptation to publish it. Furthermore, why weren't you leaving the fair with the contract for your husband happy about reuniting with him? Why were you so drawn to your ex-husband without exchanging any word? And involving me the next day in some major emotional hassle? I would feel sorry if that book would function as a trigger for destruction, but this text certainly cannot be held accountable as a reason.

Mail: Laetitia, you asked me something I couldn't properly understand and answer to. I like to know what you were asking me that evening and if we can establish at least some form of communication that

merely tells us each other things about each other.
Mail: Sebastian, you endanger my marriage.
Mail: Laetitia, you endanger it yourself, those
cultural rules on your continent do they work so
strict that they allow no extra-marital talk with
continents in-between? They certainly are not! Was
that second-long closeness between us so intimate
that it destroyed any possibility for non-intimate
contact?
Mail: Sebastian, that contact will let degrade
something else, I know it, I can feel it.
Mail: Laetitia, only if you or I let it degrade.
Again, why not apply a bit of discipline and things
may work out better than expected?
Mail: Sebastian, I fought for acceptance and a form
of relative stability of my life here, I do not want
to endanger this for just exchanging a few lines of
potentially compromising talk.
Mail: Laetitia, could you see a margin for
a professional communication or at least a
communication that does not go down in a sea of
fear of whatever kind? You trusted me as much as
to allow such a moment of closeness to develop at
that Sunday. Why can't you trust me to handle such
a communication with responsibility? You saw that I
waited three weeks before contacting you, and I think
the following sequence of letters did not compromise
you personally or in front of others. Don't you
trust yourself?
Mail: Sebastian, what do we have each other to tell
that will not fuel emotions? I could give away
information that endangers my well-being. I gave
you trust and confidence, and you asked for more.
Mail: Laetitia, giving trust and confidence certainly
does not mean that I have the right of pushing you

into areas you do not want to go, but maybe you could
at least acknowledge that I think I tried carefully
to establish a relation that won't destruct existing
ones, but neither destruct a future friendship or
whatsoever may develop from this. I cannot instigate
you to any form of communication I liked to have with
you, but taken the incoherences I have experienced,
naturally I will check a range of channels until I
have exhausted my ingenuity of producing channels
and stop, or I try until I have found a form of
interaction that gives me an explanation for those
incoherences. I offered you twice to break the
business relation, thereby cleanly leaving me without
any personal relation to you; since you ignored these
offers, I have to assume that you didn't want to
cut completely whatever ties existed. Laetitia, you
already showed such an acumen of evasion in the first
letters, where you simply ignored unwanted questions.
If you feel compromised by such sentences, why not
answer explicitly "Please Not." Do you know a secret
that forces you to see channels of business, of
emotion, of friendship amalgamated? And again,
physical distance automatically opens a limited
range of interaction. Do emotions have to disturb
any line of action; do you have to let yourself
inundated by them or do you need to exterminate
their cause? Why not try to uncouple actions and
emotions --- is that impossible? But I will not ever
go into any form of competition or fight. Whatever
kind of relation we have, this connection has to
exist on the level of two persons who are able to
choose and react freely with each other. Whereas
asymmetric relations usually load a burden on one
side; sometimes associating moral categories to
this; sometimes making those persons share blame and

reproach. This I do not want! --- When after some
initial contact one may try to establish a relation,
that relation may fail on one level, why must the
contact be severed on all levels? Unless of course
the person who severs contact completely distrusts at
least one of the two. All the best from Sebastian.

. . .

Sebastian: Maybe I bullied you too much. Again no limit-
ing answer, neither a minimal interest in any contact. You
really confuse me; these feelings-first-thinking-later views
turn things upside down. And you begin to make me feel
exhausted again. Why does speaking to you turn out to
become such a stressful act, as if walking hours through the
surf of a high tide.

Balance

Laetitia: I cannot remember of such an intense feeling of
ambiguity, not only of emotions towards two persons at one
time; but also in pure reasoning. A few weeks ago, a close
friend of mine found an aphorism and read it to me, apparently pondering to read this sentence to her boy-friend
too, without knowing how it would affect me: "You will
perceive nobody as truthful to yourself as long as you do
not perceive yourself truthful to yourself." Then she left for
her home, apparently attributing a line of reasoning to this,
certainly different from the emotions this sentence evoked in
me. Old words in a new setting can change their meaning
so profoundly or can become so crisp clear in their original

meaning, that one wonders how language enables people to relate without having to cope with more misunderstandings. What I longed to find through contact and networks with others, not only truthfulness; I have first to develop for myself, alone. This I know and always knew very well, from not too pleasant experiences. Others, even parents or husbands form a poor extension of oneself. Maybe boys get better prepared for that kind of self-reliance, because they generally focus on competition and gaining respect as an individual, not as a group-member.

Men who are able to do things completely alone always have intrigued me, maybe because this type of man really wouldn't need me. And only if such a man really wanted me, he would value me for myself, not for his need of me. (I wonder if that works the other way round too.) Nevertheless, I think I will take the risk of establishing a regular contact with you, again.

Sebastian: What kind of infatuation or love keeps alive a relation of the mutual, cooperative and friendly kind? Certainly one that acknowledges the strong element of trust. Trust allows to release control and permits the other to exert power autonomously. Nevertheless, trusting another person may still prevent that person from access to central views or structures of thought and feeling, therefore affiliation may involve more than a certain amount of trust and closeness. Non-autonomy in trust and closeness easily destroys relations, but does this non-autonomy also characterize developing relations? Do developing relations always cause this insecurity as a transitional side-effect? Or should one have an indifferent attitude to painful strains on an affiliation process. Then, only strains knowingly or unnecessarily produced by one part of the couple for testing the other's inclination need to be taken as an alarm-sign of social damage. You severed by force and severed by trying the "is that book written in some other language"-sleight instead of using my voluntary offer to stop or delay the business process. If I had to see only me, I should feel humiliated or enraged. A little rage could free me, but at the cost of striving to see some truth, something good.

And yet I wonder if my self-conditioning towards keeping a more or less respectful indifference represents a viable approach? Yes, this could be right for the right people, leading to a cooperative contact; and this could prove right with the wrong people, leading to an early break off. No, if it solely produces a mutual break down, especially in the light of some sayings like "The opposite of love is indifference, not hate.". But I hope they meant irresponsible indifference.

Laetitia: I will apologize to him and if he accepts it, it's all over and I'm free. Let's do it fast and quickly by telephone:

Laetitia: "Hello Sebastian."
Sebastian: "Hello Laetitia. —"
Laetitia: "I'm sorry."
Sebastian: "I'm just happily listening to your voice."
Laetitia: "..."
Sebastian: "The moment you thought you lost sovereignty you began shoving me away."
Laetitia: "When was that?"
Sebastian: "The moment you left the group at the hotel. Before you have been nice to me, you haven't had that cold distance."
Laetitia: "I was involved more that you might imagine."

Communicate

Laetitia: "I will return this year to the book-fair and to the same hotel. We could meet and talk. But please, I anticipate this to become a fatiguingly demanding exchange. So should I like to stop this talk now, could we stop it? Please?"
Sebastian: "Yes. Then till then."
Laetitia: "Bye."

. . .

Sebastian: That day the autumn sun burnt surfaces. The air was dry but not dusty. Colors gleamed. — And many time-tables disciplined people. Continually and considerably disquieted, I imagined that one of us could do some thing the other could not handle satisfactorily and both of us would break down eventually. Additionally I tore myself up between not knowing how you would react and whether you would decide to enter more into my life than I could realistically expect from you. And how to anticipate my share of responsibility in devising pathways to real life, disaster or happiness, or maybe even an enduring friendship. — What did I expect anyway? What do I want and what will I get? Will this end up in two persons who want to play adult and end up in profanities?

Laetitia: Why do I have to meet you? I am meeting you totally unprotected. You have seen enough of me to crush me by using an entire list of items against me. Why do I have to take those beatings always from those I value most. It's wicked, the people I try to bind to me are those who do not like me or don't recognize me and loathe me for what

I feel I represent. The more I try to convince them of my good sides the more they seem to uncover my bad ones, as always. And as always I let this happen to me out of some strange impulse. Now the initial hope of once finding a person that values me in my entirety seems to have degraded into some masochistic ritual of mine. But that is not true. But must attachment always be executed to its bitter end?

Sebastian: There it is again, the fear that this will turn out as an elaborate strategy of yours of slowly bringing me down. Down to where and down for what? I rightfully resist to only consider that you just do it for the sake of seeing me helplessly wound up in your strangely contradicting ties. Unable to move and an easy game for anybody free to serve ones need of feeling superior. Some people relish in making aloof people helpless. But I don't think I tried to impress you with an aloof attitude, so in the worst of cases you will see some idiot and I will not do anything to free you from your opinion that I am such an idiot. You are free to act as the stone which sharpens my blade of perception not the stone that will crush me, because I will encounter you already in that infamous crushed state of mind I use so often with people who try to undercut me, so nothing may surprise me. Act like a flounder made of stone encaged in an emotional slaughterhouse.

Laetitia: I hesitated entering the restaurant in which we had stayed a year ago. Would it turn out better to wait for you or could it turn out better to keep you waiting for me? You made this question irrelevant, already sitting there and staring out of one of the restaurant's large window panes. That gave me time to scan you again. You looked so different from what I remembered you. Your hair was cut, naturally. Same face, same eyes, as far as I could see from where I stood. Maybe I should turn around and never come back. Maybe the place where you sat should have been filled with a void. — Now let's move and face the beating.

Sebastian: Looking out of the window, I could see some part of the restaurant floor reflected. Some movement in the window let me lower my eyes, exhale and freeze for a moment. If someone's life falls apart in the next minutes or hours I would share quite a part of responsibility for this. With some people one can get along easy, with others things can get complicated from angles previously unimaginable. Now this is navigating close to the cliffs again. Looking up I saw you looking at me, no hello, just an uneasy smile. — And you carefully sat down facing me. — Acting out the flight-reflex could have proved socially highly unbecoming.

Laetitia: Again that undefinable mixture of little boy and old man in his look. As if you have a constantly undecided setting of mind and as if you do not feel the need to decide for yourself what to think or how to act. But obviously you do not let others decide for yourself. No poker-face, but you hide yourself behind your own undecidedness, behind your own act of perceiving your counterpart. — The best thing to check the atmosphere is the following entrée: "I am sorry."
For a moment you closed your eyes.

Sebastian: Is this a test?   I do not mind being tested
out.   But I always wonder how those I would test could
react if they noticed.   So I prefer observational tests to
active testing methods.   I have a constant fear that active
tests on my side could release hell on earth and destroy a
relation.   So if you want to test test but please, if I react
again, do not make me responsible for you feeling yourself
cornered.

Sebastian: "For what?"
My god that must have sounded depressed and depressing! You just look at me questioningly.   Again this locking
of looks, I looked away and already regretting wondering
what are we doing here?
"For hiding your intelligence from me?   That's no insult,
that's at most a sign of superior intelligence." I responded,
I think in an overly tense frightful voice.   The first major
glitch.   Truthfulness is doom.

Laetitia: That's it.   Whatever you say, you cover your insult
as a compliment or vice versa.   You still cover yourself.   Now
I noticed what confused both of us so much: You covered to
protect yourself, you covered to protect me by offering me a
way out of my agent-business.   I covered to protect myself,
I did not want to hurt or to loose you.   Everyone confused
everyone else in struggling in search of some straight line for
both.   I had to suppress a laugh at that craziness.   You felt
this, I saw your bewildered look as a reaction to my smile.

Sebastian: You were derailing me again.   Truthfulness with
you seems to constantly sink one of us.   What did your
"sorriness" signify, a mere soft opening to our communication?   An apology?   An empathic statement?

"If this was meant as an apology, I have not felt insulted, so I have no reason to accept an apology. I ... , I feel sorry for something I try when striving to change the setting for the better and try to let the other feel the result. Do not complicate your life with morals that serve nobody well." What was meant to untighten the air, comes as a lecturing of confusion, the whole thing goes straight down. Stop it and let her speak.

Laetitia: That is you taking aggression and blame away from me, as done in your email. A little harshness in the matter-of-fact attitude but you strive not to overdo it. And yet exactly this makes me feel again like a little child in front of my parents, again having done somewhat inexcusable. The more you helplessly strive to help me, the more I feel the urge to hurt you and feel your pain.

And I can see your persistence in keeping soft and uncommitted; I can feel that if I really wanted to grab you, you would dodge away, you would slip away from me like a fish. So, just out of curiosity, I will try to nail him down again, now using words:

"My dear Sebastian the only clearly stated hint from you, concerning that you may see in me more than just a friend comes from a mixture of a reoccurring quirkiness of formulations, sometimes outright allusions, and a uniquely withheld but constantly practiced friendliness. Since I can hope to have established a stable relation with you, I would like to attempt another pass of curiosity: I always wondered what would mean the words 'I love you' spoken from me to you?"

Sebastian: A test. First she puts herself on a safe ground, then she tests. Now do not blow this one and don't overdo it; just give her the words she most probably would like to listen to:

"Taken literally, the infinitive alone cuts like a blade. A die cast muffling variety?   Words like this may in the worst case crystallize or mummify what actually should form or become the basis of an evolving effort on both sides.   Even if these words are sent out only as a silent message: They make people shiver, surge and inundate them, produce a jolt of feeling ultimate friendliness.   Even if you weren't married, a pervading fright of goofing the ensuing adaption process.   Pure terror, that, due to some deficiency on either side, the mutual promise implied fades in the light of time."
I took a breath.   Cold-bloodedness does not necessarily ensue cold-heartedness, but maybe this sermon didn't fit neither.

Laetitia: "But Sebastian, you dissect, you analyze out of fear; your first words suffice.   That statement is just meant to convey a feeling, not a connection.   A connection will emerge from further talk.   This sentence is not meant to make you think for both people but to ask what you feel yourself of the other one.   View these three words as the seeds for a new enriching relation.   And even if a potential for failure prevails, why not at least try to overcome its stifling effect.   You acted according to this, remember, and I acted according to this!"
"OK, let us change the subject a little; listening to the sounds you make makes me feel safe, but the things you say about us or yourself make me wonder where you are steering?"

Sebastian: "At a sort of a balance!   As I signalled in the beginning I am protecting myself, and the moment you looked at me showing yourself so unable to protect yourself and later so openly reluctant to close yourself up in an elegant way; you gave me the idea that I had to protect even yourself from yourself. This attitude of mine is just an artifact of that time." You are one of those that can make people talk like a waterfall.

Laetitia: "Do you feel safe now?"
Sebastian: Ah, some social reverse engineering! "I still don't know, maybe you will give me again some fireworks and afterwards let me stand in the dark."
Laetitia: "I am sorry, but I myself didn't know what was happening. Just your look produced an emotional mess with me. You made room for me or withdrew yourself, whatever one may interpret into it, you let me enter within yourself without showing me anything. But you did not feel empty, to the contrary ... "

Sebastian: "Your sudden change to friendliness from Saturday to Sunday made me so puzzled that I just produced that, as I think, incredulous and absorbing look; and you were the only one ever to see that look because you opened yourself. And — irresistibility attracts, but does not find counterparts ..."
Laetitia: "Now, alone to be able to talk to you feels incredible."
Sebastian: "The more we talk the more you might see traits in me you do not like, the more you may become turned down."
Laetitia: "That works in both ways and consciously."
Sebastian: "Ugh? Ah!"

Laetitia: "You may impress me, you may alienate me; I may do the same with you and we both may continue to use that as a method to keep distance."

Sebastian: "Keeping a balance?"

Laetitia: "Is it then again a game we play?"

Sebastian: "Just keeping up communication?   — Why shouldn't we try to establish a balanced relation of whatever kind as long as both sides stay halfway happy?"

Laetitia: "Then what we have could pass as a form of friendship doesn't it?"

Sebastian: "Yes, if you want this to become that.   Since I see you in a situation much more difficult than mine, I will try to uphold any kind of friendly form of communication that pleases you."

Laetitia: "You do not open yourself, you are covering yourself again."

I regretted my annoyedly resounding tone immediately, either you didn't notice the tone or you ignored it again.   I began wondering at what time your social embrace would brake and your graceful attitude would change into a squeeze — as usual.

Sebastian: "You didn't cover yourself as we met and receded.   Nevertheless you wanted me to uncover.   The whole relation deteriorated that way almost before it had begun."

Laetitia: Does the squeeze begin now?

"But ... what did you see in me, and what do you see in me now?"

Sebastian: You look worrisome, what did I do again? Trying to keep you poised or only facing you balanced always makes me feel responsible.

" ... I do not think you want a list of attractive features of

yourself or a list of reservations of mine concerning your behavior. You might still ask me the question: Is he still worth
the trouble or should I dump him right now and here? And
why does he invest that much time in trying to assess the
character of a person he should have dumped a long time
ago?"

Laetitia: Where is he going now? Will you tear me to pieces
now?

"You love me?"

Sebastian: "I rather prefer to fear you! You want to get me
exposed! I fear you asking such direct questions that again
may let both of us fall apart!"

Laetitia: "You avoid the core of your feelings."

Sebastian: "Why do you so insistingly want to uncover me?"

Laetitia: "Because I think that Sunday afternoon I unfortunately had let you see right into me."

Doesn't he want to tell me because there is nothing to tell,
or does he really hide out of some fear?

Sebastian: "I cannot remember having ever seen a face expressing at least two different feelings like apprehension and
curiosity, friendliness and subtleness so intensely as yours. I
think I only could see somewhat more because we have some
kind of a similar background of a view onto things. Therefore, I suspect that a large part what I 'saw' could turn out
as just a reflection, a resonance of myself. Maybe I . . .
we exchanged thoughts about things so highly abstracted
from individual experience, that these topics could named
'mutual view' or so, maybe by talking together we would
find a lot of similarities. So, much of the core you search
in me may already exist in yourself."

Laetitia: "You show me an expert in dodging questions. You may have a well-developed command of words and thoughts but you use them also to hide behind them."

Sebastian: "Seeing solely that kind of abstracted core of 'I love you' already has lead to a lot of trouble. Why do you insist on words of me, why doesn't your observation answer your question, even in a much richer way. If you allow, let us consider a less abstract question concerning your core question. What do men and women do most of their time if they live in a marriage-like relation? —
They speak to each other, they talk, they practice coopera-tive behavior, they reassure, they help each other — ideally."

Laetitia: "This may not come from loving each other."
Sebastian: "This may enrich a relation but it need not found the relation. And I think you know best what difficulties may arise when founding a relation on love and that real love seldom unveils itself through the use of words."
Laetitia: "But why can't you speak about your feelings to me?"
Sebastian: "They might embarrass you and you could with-draw again. As you withdrew because of yours. And the spoken word might destroy a possible bond between us that I value highly and of which I hope that you give that bond a meaning beyond some business relation. At least I hope that I'm more than an emotional business relation to you."
Laetitia: "You knew from the beginning."
Sebastian: "I suspected, you confused me terribly."
Laetitia: "I feel sorry."
Sebastian: "Partly I confused myself. I'm doing most of the talk again. Again I have the feeling that you do the main

work in sizing me up."

Laetitia: Smiling, "I am a weak woman, I need to protect myself."

Sebastian: "But I won't act out a complement for you. And those women who stress their weakness usually end up as a very strong counterpart, a very good sign." Smiling back.

Laetitia: "You grin like a little boy and speak like an old man, again confusing me now. I still wonder if you want to build me up with that talk or if you believe it yourself. You cannot happen to act that good, is this a test?"

Sebastian: "You try to make me say things explicitly to reassure you. But even then you also stay on your side. So why do you want me to put in words what you already feel."

Laetitia: "Am I safe with you?"

Sebastian: "— Considering the weakness of words in these cases, could the past serve as proof? — I don't like promising, but me myself feeling as a creature of habit and self-conditioning, I hope that as long as you do not blast me away with some concoction of yours, I will strive to not embarrass you or endanger your marriage by actively causing problems. — How does that make you feel?"

Laetitia: "Our main contact will happen through writing, so there is enough time to get over the stress of personal meetings ... "

Sebastian: "Does this stress you?"

Laetitia: "I know I will do a lot of thinking afterwards. Certainly, about chances lost and about how risks taken might really develop for the better. How long waiting is prudent and where hesitating hampers living. Which decision improves life and which one makes life more difficult. That goodwill often is wasted on the wrong persons and rigidity the same. Goodwill and rigidity, both, seem to add up each other in precisely the wrong directions. —"

Sebastian: "But if cleared by speaking about these things, with harnessed emotional involvement, one can retain trust and confidence. This seems to me a better solution than a cutoff on all communicational levels. Now this here may require self-discipline, but exactly this should occur as central aspect of any kind of civilized view of others ..."

Laetitia: "And if one person gets into trouble, the other could help without exploiting weaknesses, but rather protect both sides from errors, don't you think so?"

Sebastian: "We could try such an approach to each other becoming stable and working, but I don't want to fool you, there exists still more than simple friendship with me."

Laetitia: "Finally you spare me only a glimmering. If each of us knows how to manage each other's emotions ... That's fine with me. But we should organize those meetings sparingly."

I still suspect that you really blank away emotionally whenever you can, even now I get the impression that from time to time you have complete emotional black-outs. And yet the friendly atmosphere around you stays, like a constant surf on a shoreline. Only the larger waves seem to miss, even during heavy gusts of wind, thunder and rain. A pacific ocean in a person.

Sebastian: "And maybe I can offer you an answer to my strangely undecided attitude: I try to keep my emotional channel free from reasoning and social responsibilities. This lets me experience emotions, as I hope, as every other person. But then, in parallel, my reasoning tries to analyze and to project, as if assessing some chess constellation, trying to concentrate and to keep any emotional firestorm away from that channel. Thus becoming able to interact socially for the best of all associated people including me, but never excluding others deliberately. This may sound great, but most of the time I train myself, fear failure, balance ridges, run blades and muse in the meantime about improving my social performance. So don't mistake the words and the program for the action, I'm afraid I already do this too often." — And now present as an underlying view but consciously only recalled later — Considering this whole relation in hindsight five or ten years in the future, I should become aware that I did not try to intimidate the other one, and that I did understand the actions of the other as not meant to be felt intimidating either. Both should finally understand themselves as having been watching and acting with the intent of not hurting others or oneself. And if some action proved dysfunctional, then as having strived to be able to tolerate this with the other and with oneself and having sought *for both* some form of relief.

Laetitia: "Now this explains something. This compartmentalization of yours seemed really to work with me, I was totally confused by your strange reactions. And therefore with you, the notions closeness and intimacy waver between working either as synonyms or appearing as antonyms." A very interesting constellation because you seem to place stability of a relation over the nature of a relation, be it friendship or else. That allows to backtrace former experiences of yours: Apparently someone left you very helpless once and now you strive more or less helplessly to protect — yourself — and other people you value. If this contains truth, I could feel completely safe with you. But still — let's see, I shouldn't, rather I needn't let any guards down!

Sebastian: "You too protected yourself, why do you expect for me a differing attitude?"

Laetitia: "I opened myself to you."

Sebastian: "You determine your extent, I determine mine; neither me nor you have the right to apply force in letting the other become more open. You acted carefully, I tried to act carefully. And though we came from different ends, we are talking now. — Comparing with some former situations this still amazes, awes me."

Laetitia: "Ridiculing me again?"

Sebastian: "I do not ridicule you when I speak of my emotional impressions using my words."

Laetitia: "So ... So you are in awe speaking to me?"

Sebastian: "It's nice sitting here and having the impression to be able to really talk to you. And sensing that the other too wishes to make this talk a pleasant one. This produces the same happiness in me as that Sunday when I witnessed how you three women let virtually bloom such a nice atmosphere around them."

Laetitia: "You like that — listening to women talking?"

Sebastian: "I like seeing happy people together."

Laetitia: "Are you unhappy or alone?"

Sebastian: — "You exert the force of a friendly sea-shell opener.

I wonder what would happen to a man who would question a woman that nosily. — But to answer the question as truthful as possible: As far as I can say, if there should exist traits of loneliness or unhappiness in me, curiosity and work definitely outweigh these traits."

Laetitia: "Do you dodge my question?"

Sebastian: "You are interrogating me as if you want to wring me out! Working alone, I have the opportunity of doing something myself. This enables me to become happy with myself. Together with others, especially in an agreeable atmosphere like this one, I can enjoy the presence and the exchange with others. This enables me to become happy with other people too. So I try to get the best out of various situations. These are just rather generally formulated paths to the feeling of contentment with oneself and others."

Laetitia: "You open yourself to emotions of others but not to your own ones. Therefore it seemed to me that you played emotional hide and seek with me."

Sebastian: "If not needed, why should my emotions influence my actions. 'Hide and seek' may translate to avoid obliging you or loosing myself. And may I be allowed to show my consideration using my ways, as you handled it your way?"

Laetitia: "But your way means two way talk and one way analysis, I do not want to be made to object of even a continuous considerate scrutiny."

Sebastian: "As I said, I just separate observation and action, this does not harm anybody. And I think you did not feel uncomfortable with me as I did exactly that on that Sunday. And frankly I had the impression that your emotions completely sufficed to complicate the situation. If I had acted showing you mine too, each of us would have narrowed down any option of reaction to just one or two rather radical ones. Obviously you refrained from that your way and I tried to avoid this my way. Now, I hope we have found some means to circumvent emotion destroying communication and therefore I feel some hope for steadiness between us two building inside me. But I equally hope that even this emotion does not put me off guard."

Laetitia: "Do you like me? I like very much what I have seen of you. But you shouldn't forget we know each other very little. And I wonder whether we like only what we already know or do recognize in others. Maybe we are not capable of opening ourselves to really different persons as long as we search for the one and only ideal partner with whom we can correspond perfectly. By that we may only meet ourselves."

Sebastian: "Whom we meet in another person should become interesting, but not crucial, as long as both are able to correspond to each other ..."

Laetitia: "Yes, I know they have to have this same humanistic base as you told."

Sebastian: "Yes, infatuation and romantic love may supplement this pleasantly, but I think they need that base to stabilize the connection. Unless of course there are other more profane bases for stabilizing relations."

Laetitia: "There needs to prevail a basic dependability and cooperativeness among people who want to establish any kind of social relation. Any kind of love and even romantic love draws its strength from that base. If that base can deteriorate or absent itself too many a time, then the whole relation will fall apart sooner or later. Love seems to extend friendship in that it accepts whatever comes from the other be it good or bad. But I have seen too much of that to hope for happy endings."

Sebastian: "I hope that you see love a tint too fatalistic."

Laetitia: "What about sex?"

Sebastian: "You try to test me again? Giving me a cliff to navigate onto, or is that still curiosity?" (By hitting a bull's eye you evade the bull. How nice, how exhilarating, you really try to fence with me, you have stopped buzz-sawing me!)

Laetitia: "Just answer!"

Sebastian: "You are safe, I think we have strained each other enough so far."

Laetitia: "How safe?"

Sebastian: "Safe enough because your words exhaust me. If I would feel that tired having double my age, I would feel old." Attempting a weak careful smile, but realizing your demanding look, I tried to adhere to your field of interest. — "One should want it if one knows the other wants it out of a free choice. That's the double paradox that has to be solved when incrementally establishing a good relation, isn't it?". You seemed satisfied but not relieved.

Laetitia: "Anyway, at times free will and emotion already seem a paradox enough! But I still suspect that you tell me things I want to hear and you even may act according to this."

Sebastian: "So things won't get easy, won't they?"

Laetitia: "No, but ... , we will see ... together."

Her Letter about Intimate Correspondence

My dear Sebastian,
After these months of talking to you, I have compiled
some ideas I remembered we discussed and I have added
some of my own notes:

I still recall, long ago, most vividly standing within a group
of fellow art and literature students at the university book
shop, reuniting after the term break.   They continually,
and at times most pleasantly, talked about whom they had
acquainted and what other interesting things had happened
to them and their friends in the mean-time. All of a sudden
I stood there perplexed, unable to further follow any talk,
really stunned, when I realized that sweet talk, marriage or
sex do not relate in the least to real intimacy between people.   I kept wondering what really keeps people together,
what really binds them?   Romanticism?   Simply a daily
routine, material security?   Hard excruciating mutual experiences, fear of loss, fear of loneliness? The wish of seeing
in the other a piece of oneself?   Or having the other reassuring the importance of one's own presence to him, just
the feeling of being wanted?   Maybe all that can lead to
closeness and intimacy between people; but I wondered if
one could find, at least partially, an underlying and uniting
idea.   Probably my doubts originated from having seen so
many failed examples for all these ways to closeness.   These
ways seemed only means to me not ends, but what are the
ends?   Is one end a mutually reassured, viable and stable
peace of mind of both?

Unique intimate moments, which I remember most clearly,
occurred as unexpected bridgings of communicational gaps:

If in a quarrel with my husband our eyes met and this immediately and noticeably attuned the heated atmosphere with both of us. The look I once exchanged with a mother in an airport lounge, a total stranger; she was feeding her baby. The last moments I had together with my father, which finally made it possible to speak without that ever-lasting authoritarian air of his. And the final moment as our eyes met that afternoon.

First, I gathered that closeness meant feeling understood, accepted as a whole. Being able to make the other feel comfortable and safe as a person. A promise of a sort of unique social relation that provides a bit of exclusiveness, even when living together with family and friends. Maybe by doing things together, talking to each other, developing some mutual reassurance and, if necessary, consolation. If I remember this properly, I think marriage extended these ideas. Thoughts and views touched each other, we shared strengths and weaknesses, borrowed strengths to ease weaknesses. At times we could reflect feelings until they became purified from any profane context. And there were few moments of feeling the other feel oneself. Does life promise more?

Closeness, maybe seen also in the sense of having the faculty of mutually concentrating on each other, of shutting the world out. And correspondence heightening the feeling of closeness by seeing or discovering mutual similarities, communicating in accord. By recreating such moments and then falling back into oneself, living through recollections, each one develops the reassurance of a stable relation. Sometimes men already appear to feel happy with the closeness of doing something together without much communication, I wonder if they would call this closeness or even correspondence. Husbands reoccurringly develop an expertise in mixing these things up and thereby confusing their wives. I always have wondered if this kind of "keeping the women busy" comes consciously to their minds or if that is just a remnant of their boyhood where they kept their mothers busy.

Nevertheless, as far as I can see now, I think one could state the following without going too wrong: Love acts only as a director on intimacy, friendship and human inclination in general; on patience, tolerance and empathic behavior. The more these small parts of contacting and getting along with people develop, the more love can successfully direct a relation. People tormented by perceived or real restraining forces, like shame, fright, moral anticipations; those people who have been deprived from learning the little constructive social skills get chased into a social swamp by even such a serene emotion as love. I had to learn this myself; only few treasured acquaintances of mine, by merely giving a good example, demonstrated or taught me a variety of those refined social skills. And from time to time I fall back into the old panic of loosing bonds with people whom I have learned to like and who seem to disintegrate before my eyes like dust and thereby making me feel the same.

The following advice was given to me by an elderly woman, to whom I unfortunately could speak only a few hours. By own experience I know how emotions may interfere with that piece of advice and I am afraid that I did outrightly ignore that advice too often. Maybe the written form of that advice gives it more authority, gives it more truth or a more compelling air: If making a person a friend (or later a spouse), imagine if you had to decide whether this prospective friend was a good choice for your best friend, so ask yourself: "Would this prospective friend produce a happy and stable relation with my best friend?" Could you let them affiliate themselves without any reservation? Have you had a thought beginning with "but actually ... " or "if that would be taken seriously ... " or the like? Does there reoccur any uneasiness when spending time together? What set of adverbs, not adjectives, describes this relation so far and what adverbs make it differ from other relations? And overall remember that good manners basically only require a good actor, a friendly view on life and on people in general has to be assessed by other means.

I remember when I was a small girl wondering about the others who had these smooth manners, now I can see that many of those smooth manners or mannerisms could pass as imitational acting. But proficiency in good showmanship can bring one advantage: A really good showperson tries to assess to whom he or she is speaking, thereby sensing and feeling the counterpart. But many people loose this skill and fall into isolated egocentrism, then into self-deception and ensuing depression. Still, even real authenticity, also when well developed, always has to cope with failure, error and degradation. But this closeness to oneself, more than anything else, opens life's doors to experience and learning. This does not make life easy and safe, but it saves oneself from routine and senselessness. And as I noticed last year, even then own experiences may surprise oneself more than one could have been expected.

Though one look exchanged between two persons can hold the promise of intimacy, closer than that of many married couples, that promise also can be kept by both without acting this out unconditionally. Rather, using this promise as a secure basis for slowly approaching each other. For making any adaptation to each other less straining and leaving everybody enough room for negotiating with oneself and with the other one. Temperedly acting out one's emotions keeps an immense emotional tension coupled with a sense of trust and confidence that could not build up otherwise. But sometimes holding such a balance becomes simply impossible. Especially if one finds a partner who takes willingly part in such gradual association, then this partner shows thereby that he has no fear exposing some of his more unadvantageous traits. At the same time, those who try to protect, not hide, themselves may also seriously consider to loose themselves or give themselves.

Even before my first marriage, close friends made it possible for me to witness the beginning, the happiness and the degradations of relations. The stable relations always impressed me as a consanguinity of pure magic. Now I suspect that the stability of a marriage depends more on mutual correspondence than on any sorts of idealized love. Whether the responsibility for establishing and caring for that correspondence has been evenly apportioned, whether one notices voluntary or compulsory traits or characteristics, may remain another question. In the worst cases I saw stability just assured by material well-being and adherence to convention, a truly depressing perspective. I witnessed relations where each side got some minimal emotional or material service out of the other, however warped and tilted the rest of that relation may have appeared, some of the the most strange constellations produced a remarkably stable bond. But considering my own experience, the stability seems to root in a day-to-day correspondence, which of course gets most dearly enhanced by openness, poise, trust and love. I could not find means that assure success, neither ends that assure success. Any couple seems bound to work out the core of their relation alone, usually there comes weak or no help from outside, as so often in life. Finding here a working path overcomes one of the bigger challenges to one's individuality. If you don't want, no authority can take that away from you! Generally speaking, I guess, both have to find some stability in their own lives before they unite, then they might have a better chance to stabilize their mutual relation too. Such a relation then becomes a living creature itself, to be fostered and reassessed caringly by both. And yet, even if both strive to do the best they can, that creature may perish miraculously, as I could experience myself. Of course supporting friends and dear relatives may help, but all this serves little if both cannot balance out themselves, individually and together.

Also remembering the strangely interlocked and interwoven relation of my parents, before they separated; my second surprise, once during my second marriage, gave a realization about myself. I felt that I would hardly ever have a real intimate relationship with anyone unless I valued myself first, in a non-intimidating way, keeping respect for myself and especially keeping respect for others. This meant also that I rather had to work on myself, mainly thereby gaining more influence on me managing my relations. Later the so-called daily necessities and the need to coherently associate with immediate surroundings often infringed the effective transfer of this insight into action.   Nevertheless, the first effect I clearly noticed was that I evaded others working on me, thereby averting me from pleasing them by adapting and confining myself to their necessities.   And to my continually growing fascination, aided by some friendly evasion and some friendly determined resilience of mine, things improved, relations got better and gradually life got happier.   Explicitly voicing my wishes concerning myself without either anticipatively trying to evade or dodge the other's line of power, now got me out of more problems than my introverted defensiveness got me into tensions before.   I still act out naturally and friendly, but I don't need to convince other persons of me, I don't need to fear their aggression, neither do I have to feel connected to people so much as to vindicate my personal decisions.   I ask for help, if necessary, but I decide eventually; I don't need to await affirmative movements from others that allow me to proceed with my actions.   Overall, I try to keep unwanted influences outside myself; ideally those irritations should loose any sort of compulsory effect on me.   Though that kind of extensive freedom turned out to have an highly incremental character, I did draw confidence from my increased well-being.   Few already lost relations broke, but most relations improved most amicably.   Thus having stabilized myself I could apologize myself as I could excuse others much easier without feeling a loss of respect in both directions.   I found myself by stopping to search for others; and yet now, to those I value, I have a stronger relation than ever before.

Sebastian,
maybe you would care to re-read the text, change my

propositions, extend them or reassess them if you
consider it sensible. Would you then please return
them for revising? If you consent, we could ponder to
try to publicize this work. Of course the text misses
some intimate or harsher thoughts and speculations of
both sides which have been told each other much later,
way after the production of this compilation. But I
think that the remaining thoughts leave the essence of
the exposed communication basically unchanged.

Fortunately this story found an happy end, which one and
to what extend cannot be specified here, because the de-
tails would give away compromising information. Still any
resemblance to living or non-living persons happens to appear fully coincidental and without intent or purpose. The
names Laetitia and Sebastian were chosen completely at
random.